Cara ran as though pursued by the Devil. Her lungs were near bursting when Julian's arm snaked out, swinging her feet off the ground as he hauled her back against his chest. He was filled with exhilaration at his triumph, his senses quivering with a heightened awareness. As his fingers touched the burnished tresses, they dug in, and with his other hand he grasped the girl's body in a hard embrace.

The girl gasped, and he felt the whisper of air on his cheek before he lowered his mouth to her parted lips.

Blue-green eyes, flashing fire, assailed him as he gasped in recognition.

"Miss Farraday!"

PROXY BRIDE

Martha Jean Powers

FAWCETT CREST • NEW YORK

A Fawcett Crest Book
Published by Ballantine Books
Copyright © 1987 by Martha Jean Powers

Library of Congress Catalog Card Number: 87-90775

ISBN 0-449-21293-9

Manufactured in the United States of America

First Edition: August 1987

To Bill:
For friendship, trout fishing, and Maui nights.

Chapter One

"I wish I were dead."

"Nonsense, Caroline. Where's your backbone?" the duchess of Landglower snapped.

"But I've never even seen this Lord Wilton. What if he's repulsive?"

"Your marriage, my dear child, is unquestionably legal," the duchess announced. "It was conducted three months ago in my own household with duly authorized witnesses. I stood as proxy for you in this instance."

"Couldn't it be annulled?"

"Impossible!" came the adamant reply.

"Oh, Grandmother," Cara moaned, "I wish that I had never left America."

Her elegant eyebrows arched in surprise, Liela, duchess of Landglower, inspected the fiery creature who had stormed into her presence an hour earlier. Her faded blue eyes noted the defiant bearing of the young figure pacing restlessly across the thick Aubusson carpet. With a final adjustment of the lacy nightcap covering her nearly white hair, Liela leaned forward in her chair and stared piercingly at the girl.

"Caroline, I would appreciate it if you would just kindly sit down. Not only do you rouse me in the middle of the night but now proceed to make me seasick with your constant pacing."

Recognizing the steel beneath the dryly spoken rebuke, Cara flounced down ungraciously onto the chair across from her grandmother. Even in her frustrated anger the girl was practical enough to realize that she could not afford to incur the older woman's wrath. Impatience for action and a ready tongue might have been considered fine attributes for an American, but Caroline was finding that they were definitely not an asset in London in 1814.

Arms resting on her knees, hands clasped in silent supplication, Cara leaned toward the duchess.

"My marriage really can't be legal, Grandmother," Cara pleaded reasonably. "After all, I've never even set eyes on Lord Wilton."

"Now, my child, there are certain facts that must be accepted." The duchess held up one elegant blue-veined hand, curtailing the younger girl's outburst. "First, the marriage is totally, incontestably, valid."

The blunt words hit Cara like a blow. She leaned against the velvet chair back, trying to catch her breath. Her lovely white face went even paler, except for angry spots of color showing up high on her cheeks. The duchess watched with approval as the girl fought to keep her emotions under tight control. Except for her color and the thinning of her lips, Caroline's expressionless face effectively masked her inner turmoil. Her father had done well raising the child, Liela admitted.

Giving the girl time to absorb the irrefutable fact of her marriage, Liela reached for the Waterford decanter and poured sherry into two delicate crystal glasses. Raising the glass, she appraised the chit who had had the temerity to cross the ocean in the middle of a war and storm her household, rousing the duchess from a sound sleep. Knowing the rigidity of her servants, Liela suspected the latter took more nerve than the ocean crossing.

2

Her granddaughter was tiny in stature but exquisitely proportioned. She had a full bosom, accentuated by the cut of her silk dress, which, although modestly high-necked, was drawn in beneath her breasts. The black skirt fell in a shimmering flow of fabric, caressing the willowy curves of her body. Angry color burned across the girl's cheekbones in striking contrast to the almost translucent color of her skin.

"When your father proposed this marriage, I turned the entire project over to my man of business, to be sure there was nothing havey-cavey about the arrangements," the duchess continued. "It was all done with the utmost legality. I can give you no hope in that quarter, Caroline."

"I tried to convince Poppa that none of this was necessary," Cara moaned. "But he was so sick at the time that I just didn't have the heart to fight him."

"Even on his deathbed your father was only thinking of your safety and welfare, child," Liela reasoned softly.

"Oh, Gran, I can understand what he was trying to do. It's just that . . ."

Cara's voice wavered and she fought to keep her emotions intact.

"I've always known that I wouldn't have a great deal to say about the man I would marry. But to be married to a man I've never even set eyes on is appalling."

"My dear child, you can't be expecting love?" the duchess objected vigorously.

"Well, you did, Gran," Cara accused the older woman.

Taking advantage of her grandmother's discomfort, Cara plunged ahead. "As I recall the story, you were already betrothed to the son of a wealthy landowner when Grandfather came along. You fell in love with him, and when your parents refused to allow you to break the engagement, you decided to elope to Gretna Green." Cara's eyes twinkled mischievously into her grandmother's watery blue ones. "If I remember correctly, you were in your nightgown."

3

Two spots of color shone on the wrinkled cheeks of the older woman. "At least you should get the story correct," she snapped.

A gentle smile played across the features of the old woman as she remembered a time when her blood had pulsed as vibrantly as her granddaughter's. She had loved Paxton from the first day that she had seen him.

"Actually I was fully dressed, but it was late at night when I stole out of the house and rode to your grandfather's estate. He promptly saddled a horse and accompanied me back home, where he awakened the household. While my father ranted and threatened, Paxton listened calmly, and then he announced that, in view of my compromised position, he would gladly marry me. He was a fine man, your grandfather."

There was silence in the room except for the gentle crackle of the logs burning in the fireplace. The duchess stared into the flames, remembering the passion ignited by her husband. Absently she turned the large encrusted ducal ring on her finger.

"What would you have me do, Cara?"

Touched that her grandmother had finally used her pet name, Cara flung herself at Liela's feet, reaching up to hold the long, elegant hands of the older woman.

"Couldn't I just go away, Gran? You could say that I never arrived and that, for all you know, I am dead."

"Oh, my dear, life is never that simple. You can't just run away. You would have no life at all. No. It is quite impossible."

Cara put her head in her grandmother's lap, and without thought, the old woman smoothed the riot of reddish-gold curls that tumbled down the girl's back. The duchess smiled as her hands touched the fiery tresses, remembering her own once-red hair. Against her knee Liela could feel the heartbeat of the distraught child. Each beat thudded dolefully.

4

"I want to help you, but you really must see that it would not be fair to Lord Wilton to let you run away."

"Fair!" the girl flared. "None of it's fair to me."

"Cara, your father had your best interests at heart. He could have married you to anyone, but I think he chose well. Lord Wilton is young and very handsome. I'm sure he has many fine qualities." Sunk in her own despair, Cara failed to note the uncertainty of the duchess's appraisal. "Who knows? Given time you may grow to love him dearly."

"But, Grandmother, that's just the point. I don't have any time. We're already married. He'll never give me time to know him. We shall be introduced and then he'll have the right to do with me whatever he wants."

The older woman could not dismiss the note of distress in the girl's voice, nor the blushing agony in her face. She knew the girl was correct. The things she had heard about Wilton left her in little doubt that he would immediately bed the beautiful girl. Even at her advanced age, she chafed at her granddaughter's predicament.

Once more the room was silent. The two women were separated by a generation but joined by a common bond of blood. Wistfully, Liela searched the lovely features of the girl at her feet, seeing herself at the same age, filled with the passion and romance of youth. Because of her love for her husband, Liela had come joyfully to the marriage bed. She had blossomed under Paxton's gentle lovemaking. Even now she could imagine the pain and embarrassment she would have suffered if he had been a lustful stranger.

"Sit up, Cara." The duchess's voice was brisk in decision. "I cannot set this marriage aside for you. But I could arrange for you to get to know Wilton without his suspecting who you are."

"Oh, Gran," Caroline said. The bodice of her dress rose and fell rapidly as she panted in her agitation.

"No, don't hurl yourself on me." Liela held up her

hands in alarm. "Just sit quietly. If this could be arranged, would you be content to accept this marriage?"

"Have I any choice?" the girl asked dryly.

"In actual fact, no."

"Then I accept." Caroline grimaced but, with the resilience of youth, was caught up in the excitement of the proposal. "How can I meet him without Wilton's knowing who I am?"

"First, does anyone know that you have arrived in England?"

"No one except you. When I sailed, I used my mother's name. I arrived as Caroline Farraday. Bethel, my maid, came with me from America. She's English, and once war was declared between England and the United States, she wanted to return home. It was difficult in the beginning to book passage, so she was forced to wait until I was able to leave."

"And when you arrived this evening? What exactly did you do?" The duchess knew the answers to the questions, but she needed more time to formulate the partially conceived plan in her head.

"We came directly from the ship in a closed hackney. I was heavily veiled. After all, I am still in mourning. Besides, I know that I bear a strong resemblance to my father, and I was afraid of being recognized by someone on your staff. When we were admitted, I handed the sealed note to your butler and demanded that he present it to you immediately."

Liela smiled, imagining the amount of determination it must have taken to coerce her household into waking her. Her own abigail, Anna, had tiptoed in and gently shaken the duchess, expecting at any minute to incur the wrath of her mistress. The note had identified Caroline and asked that they meet in privacy to discuss a most urgent matter.

"Anna has been guarding the doors and keeping your Bethel away from the others. I would trust Anna with my

6

life. She already knows more secrets about our family than is good for her. However, I suppose one more won't kill her," the duchess finished wryly.

"You've got some kind of plan, haven't you, Gran?" Cara's eyes were alight with mischief.

"Just how much did your father tell you about Lord Wilton?"

"Not very much, really. He said he was the son of an old friend of his. I gather, since he approved of the father, he assumed the son would be a good husband." Cara winced at the final word, still unable to come to grips with the fact that she actually was married to the man.

The duchess left her chair and rummaged in the pigeonholes of an inlaid rosewood desk. Pulling out a letter, she gave a sigh of satisfaction and returned to her chair. She squinted closely at the pages for several minutes and then smiled at the curious girl.

"Lady Trehune always keeps me abreast of the latest gossip. Can't really understand why anyone would tell her anything in confidence because before you could get out the door, Netty would have told at least three people. At any rate, she has her uses when you need to know anything about the *ton*."

"She wrote you about Lord Wilton?"

"Indirectly," the duchess said, smiling at her granddaughter's eagerness. "About three years ago Lord Wilton's brother and his wife were killed in a carriage accident. There were two children, and they are wards of Wilton. They live at his country estate, and according to Netty, they are in need of a governess. Knowing of your marriage, she was delighted to inform me that their last governess left under some sort of a cloud."

"You mean that I could go there as a governess? Oh, Grandmother, what a lark!"

The girl laughed deeply, much to her grandmother's approval. She was a fine, healthy animal who seemed to appreciate a good joke. No missish girl, this one, nodded the duchess.

"Do you think you could carry it off?" Liela inquired.

"I had a perfectly awful governess after Mother died." Even now, there was a note of sadness in Cara's voice as she remembered her mother. "Madame Regenard was an absolute dragon." She jumped to her feet and strutted across the carpeting. "Should I be French? I can speak it perfectly, even though my accent is a bit awkward."

"No, child," the duchess drawled. "No one would ever take you for anything but an American."

Cara whirled in her excitement and hugged herself. She debated for a moment whether or not the proper old lady would permit herself to be hugged. Then, with a flurry of red hair, the girl catapulted herself across the room and gave her astounded grandmother a hearty kiss.

"Enough, you flighty wench." Despite the gruff voice, it was obvious that the duchess was pleased.

"It's not what I came all the way from America for, but I guess it will have to do." Good breeding and a practical nature were definite assets as Cara viewed her grandmother's proposition. "I do thank you for this, Gran. How much time will I have?"

"A month. That should be long enough for our purposes. Besides, any longer might be dangerous. All you need do is observe inconspicuously in the background. No one notices servants, so you should be safely anonymous."

"It sounds perfect, Grandmother."

"Since my own servants will be talking, I will not be able to hide the fact that you have arrived from America. However, I will put it abroad that you are still grief stricken over the death of your father and have gone into seclusion. Your maid, Bethel, will remain here, playing your part, while I send you to Wilton. We will say that my granddaughter befriended you on the ship." Liela was silent, contemplating the girl; then, as though coming to a decision, she waved at Cara. "Go to the door and bring Anna and your maid. There's a great deal to do before morning."

After a brief explanation to Anna and a stunned Bethel, the duchess set them all to work with a vengeance. It was well past midnight before the transformation of Caroline Leland, heiress, to Miss Farraday, governess, was completed.

Standing in front of the mirror, Cara winced at her image.

The only remaining clue to the lovely young lady of fashion was Cara's eyes, luminous pools of startling blue-green. Woefully she gazed in the glass at the drab creature in the shapeless black dress. The merino wool hung limply around her figure, effectively hiding the curves and giving her the look of a child dressed in her older sister's clothes. Her glorious hair had been scraped severely away from her face and braided tightly, then fastened securely at the base of her neck. A cowllike headdress covered all of her hair, tying at the back of her neck and hanging down to her waist in lifeless folds. Rice powder had been applied liberally, hiding her natural color and giving her face a bland appearance.

"Oh, Gran, I look awful," Cara groaned.

"Dreadful, isn't it," the duchess pronounced smugly. "But at least if you look like that, Wilton won't have any hesitation in hiring you. Vanity, my dear, has no place in this arrangement."

"I think you're actually enjoying all this," Cara exclaimed huffily.

"I am, child. I most definitely am." Liela chuckled as she eased herself into a chair. "There are very few pleasures left to me these days. I was just beginning to wonder if it wasn't time to stick my spoon in the wall. You've brought some excitement into my life. I think I'm going to like having you in England."

9

"Is the headdress really necessary?"

"Now, Cara, be sensible. Your hair is far too beautiful not to be noticed. Best to keep it covered. You can tell them that it's an American custom. Everyone knows how bizarre you colonials are supposed to be. Don't bristle. It's rather a dangerous game you're playing."

"I know, Gran. I'll be careful," Cara promised sincerely.

"For all your freedom in America, you've been a sheltered child. When you go to Lord Wilton's, you go as a servant with very few privileges. You will have little protection from the realities of life. It is necessary to remain inconspicuous, not only to avoid a scandal, but for your own safety. Even now, I'm not sure that this is the wisest course, Cara." The duchess worried her bottom lip in indecision.

"I'll be careful, Gran," Cara repeated soberly.

After Anna and Bethel had been dismissed to complete the altering of Cara's new wardrobe, the two women sat in front of the fire with a snack, thoughtfully provided by Anna. The duchess watched as her granddaughter ate with the enthusiasm of youth. She herself nibbled some cheese and sipped a glass of wine. She was well satisfied with the chit. Although thrust into a difficult situation, she had handled herself with courage and resilience. Liela hoped that the opportunity would work to the girl's advantage.

"I do not wish to frighten you, child, but I must warn you that exposure of your true identity would mean social disaster," Liela cautioned. "A young lady of the *ton* is allowed to do certain things in England, but to playact as a servant is not one of them. It is conceivable that you would never be received in polite society if your charade were discovered."

"But, Gran, I'm a married woman now," Cara reasoned. "Poppa said that in England I would be less confined by rules if I were married."

"That part is true, of course. As a married woman, you do have a certain amount of license. However, society would not be amused by this sort of prank. Besides, have you considered how Wilton would feel?"

"As you know, Grandmother, I have tried to think about Lord Wilton as little as possible," Cara answered dryly.

Ignoring the girl's sarcasm, Liela continued, "If Wilton saw your masquerade as a form of spying, then he might refuse you the protection of his name. If thoroughly angered, he might even institute divorce proceedings."

"I thought you said that a divorce was impossible." Cara asked in amazement.

"For you to get either a divorce or an annulment is an impossibility," came the dampening answer. "If Wilton were angry enough, he could divorce you." Then, at the considering look in her grandmother's eyes, the duchess continued, "This is not a way out, my dear. Your objection has been at the cold arrangement of the marriage, not marriage itself. A renunciation by Wilton would mean you would be finished in polite society. Both here and in America. No decent man would ever consider aligning himself with a divorced woman."

"It's not fair!" Cara exclaimed.

"You're not a child, Cara. The world doesn't have to be fair. The situation exists, and you'll just have to make the best of it."

"If only Poppa had seen reason, none of this would have been necessary."

"From his letters I know he wanted only your safety and well-being. You are an heiress. At his death you would have been alone in America, with no family to protect you from the fortune hunters and charlatans. With your beauty and your money, there would have been a bevy of suitors for your hand," Liela continued. "Your father thought that if he could arrange for you to be married and living in England, he would be doing all he could to protect you."

"I do see that, Gran." Cara sighed. "I just wish there had been another way."

"Well, there's no point in spending your time with the past. Now is the time to look forward, my dear. Tomorrow you will begin your adventure. Anna will supply you with the remainder of Bethel's clothes. If they show as little taste as the dress you are wearing, your disguise should be foolproof. As long as you behave yourself and remain safely in the background, I can see little danger of exposure."

"Yes, Grandmother," Cara agreed meekly.

For a moment the duchess thought the change of clothes and the sober hairdo had taken the spirit out of the girl, until she noticed the twinkle in the blue-green eyes and the betraying dimple in her cheek. Even in the atrocious dress, there was still a definite air about the girl that would not warrant close scrutiny.

"Caroline Farraday. It sounds perfect. Very sturdy." She smiled at the girl's moue of distaste. "In the reference I have written I have explained how you became acquainted with my granddaughter and have included the details about your life that we went over tonight. I hope this will suffice to procure the position for you. I am sure that Wilton will wish to please his future bride."

"What is Lord Wilton like?" Cara asked uneasily.

"I wondered when you would get around to asking. I'm afraid your curiosity must go unchecked. I will not tell you either the good points or the bad that I have heard and seen. You are going there to make your own appraisal, and I would not prejudice you either way. Just do your best not to disgrace me."

"Yes, Grandmother." This time the meekness was genuine, as Cara acknowledged the seriousness of her undertaking.

Long after Cara was shown to her room, she lay in the bed unable to sleep. After the long voyage and the coach trip she still felt disoriented. She had come to England determined to have the marriage set aside. She realized now the immaturity of that hope. At least, her grandmother had given her a month in which to observe her new husband. She was practical enough to accept the fact that it was beyond the bounds of reality to think she would fall in love with a stranger. All she could pray was that she would find some qualities in the man she might admire. For better or worse, Lord Wilton was her husband.

On that frightening thought, Cara slept.

Chapter Two

The coach, although reasonably well sprung, rocked Cara from side to side as it traversed the bumpy corduroy. For the hundredth time her mittened hands adjusted the unfamiliar folds of the headdress covering her hair. Dust seeped into the coach, covering her face with a fine layer of grit. Despite her excitement of early morning, she had little enthusiasm left after three hours of jolting.

As the coach swerved and the horses began to slow, Cara's heart beat a frightened tattoo.

Craning her neck for a view of Weathersfield Hall, she gaped at the grandeur of the estate. The enormous edifice stood squarely amid legions of trees, which were dwarfed by the sheer immensity of the building. Formal gardens were laid out in front of the carriage sweep. Wide, shallow steps funneled up to an enormous double-doored entrance. Any courage Cara possessed fled at the magnificence of the stone ancestral hall. There would be no need to play the timid governess; she was thoroughly cowed by her surroundings.

With a shaking hand Cara handed the duchess's letter of introduction to the imperious butler who opened the door. Her boots echoed hollowly on the marble floors as she hurried after a footman as he wound a labyrinthine path through the silent corridors. Finally they stopped before a heavily carved door.

"Miss Farraday, my lord," the footman announced in stentorian tones. He placed the letter on the desk in front of Lord Wilton and then bowed himself quietly out the door.

Cara's heart was pounding desperately against her ribs, and her knees were decidedly shaky as she stood just inside the door.

"Well, girl, get over here," Julian Weathersfield barked.

"What?"

"Don't just stand there holding up the wall. Get over in the light where I can see you."

Instinctively Cara's chin went up at his rudeness. Barely in time she remembered her grandmother's strictures, and she scurried to comply with Julian's order. Unable to withstand the baleful gaze trained on her, Cara stammered her introduction.

"The duchess of Landglower was, eh, is pleased to send me to Your Lordship to fill the position of governess."

"Pleased, was she?" Julian snorted, glowering across the desk at the youthful figure before him. "The duchess sends a child to look after my wards."

"I am not a child," Cara snapped indignantly. "I am nineteen years old, Your Lordship."

"Such an advanced age," he sneered. "Good Lord, girl, my nephew is nine. You're only ten years older."

"I believe I will be able to handle the boy. I have had a great deal of experience in those ten years."

"Oh, to be sure," Julian scoffed. "Well, sit down while I read the duchess's letter. It should prove amusing if nothing else."

"I would prefer to stand," Cara answered primly, although she would have felt much steadier anchored to a chair.

"Then stand and be quiet" was the exasperated reply.

As Julian broke the seal on her grandmother's letter, Cara was grateful for the opportunity to make her own inspection of the man who, unbelievably, was her husband.

The sheer size of the man was impressive. He was well over six feet and heavily built, although there did not appear to be an ounce of excess weight. He had the well-muscled body of an athlete, with none of the apparent dissipation so often evident in moneyed gentlemen. The fawn velvet jacket fit him like a second skin. His shirt gleamed whitely at his wrists, and his neck was bound by an intricately tied neckcloth of silk and lace. The delicacy of his cravat contrasted drastically with the aura of masculinity that emanated from the man.

"Quite finished with your inspection, Miss Farraday?" Julian asked in amusement as he looked up and noticed the girl's concentration.

"Yes, thank you, my lord."

With the pert response, Julian caught the barest flash of angry blue-green eyes before the flustered chit dropped her head to stare at the toes of her scuffed half boots.

"The duchess claims you are from America and are very used to children."

Julian's drawling voice lent skepticism to the simple statement. Clenching her teeth to keep back a sharp retort, Cara breathed deeply before she felt capable of a serene reply. "Yes, my lord." Inwardly she seethed at her inability to snap back at her inquisitor. "My last post was as governess to the Blakelys' six children."

"Then I'm sure you are well qualified to take over the care of my two termagant wards." Julian's acid tones left little doubt that he felt her capabilities fell far short of the mark.

"Do you doubt my ability?" Haughtily Cara drew herself up to her full five-foot-three height.

"Miss Farraday," Julian snapped in exasperation, "there have been four governesses in the past two years. All of them left under less than auspicious circumstances. Do you really think, with your extreme youth, you will be able to handle your charges where the others have failed?''

"I don't know," Cara answered honestly. Then, as Julian arched an inquiring eyebrow, she stuttered uncertainly. "It seems to me, that is, I believe that . . ." She ground to a halt, then summoned courage to plunge ahead. "I am quite sure I shall be able to fulfill all of my responsibilities.''

For a moment Julian had an overwhelming urge to laugh at the unflinching determination stamped on the young girl's face. He rubbed a hand across his forehead, wondering at his own patience with the exasperating child. Normally he would have quickly resolved the question instead of entering into a battle of words. There was some quality in the girl that had piqued his interest.

Silently he took a closer look at the colorless figure standing rigidly before his desk. There was nothing attractive about the bland-faced chit. He shuddered slightly at the dun-colored tweed dress that effectively muffled her body, from the tip of her stubborn chin to the toes of her boots. There was so much excess material that Julian suspected the dress would be able to stand up without anyone inside. The wimplelike headdress annoyed him, as it completely covered her hair. He had little hope the color or texture of the hidden tresses would be worth the trouble of a peek. In his various dealings with women, it was his impression that if a woman's hair was notable at all, she flaunted it in excruciatingly elaborate curls and ringlets. All in all, the girl appeared to be a nonentity, but there had been the slightest trace of defiance in her voice that gave him a moment of disquiet. Shrugging away this nonsensical feeling, Julian continued his questioning.

"Aside from music and embroidery, have you any sort of classical education that might be of some benefit to my wards?''

Once again Julian caught the merest blaze of color before the girl's eyes closed tightly, as if in pain.

"I have had a firm grounding in mathematics, astronomy, and the physical sciences. I am well versed in both ancient and modern poetry and a broad range of literature," Cara managed to grit out in a passably civil tone. "I speak and read French, Latin, and Greek. Although I enjoy music, I have absolutely no ability to play an instrument, and my embroidery work is still at the level of a four-year-old. But since these last two seem of little importance to you, I still feel that I am fully qualified to accept the position," Cara finished briskly.

Eyes narrowed to icy slits, Julian leaned forward on his elbows, staring at the flush-faced girl whose eyes were demurely downcast.

"Miss Farraday"—Wilton spoke softly, but there was an underlying shaft of steel running through his voice—"yours is not the sort of conciliating attitude expected in someone seeking a position. You seem curiously oblivious of the honor of having my wards as your charges."

"In America one does not beg for a position," Cara snapped, unable to control a flash of temperament. "We take pride in our work, no matter who employs us."

Nonplussed at the girl's impertinence, Julian could only gawk at the young woman. In all his remembrance, no servant had ever dared to speak to him in this manner. He rose to his feet, watching in satisfaction when the girl's eyes widened in fear as he towered over her diminutive figure.

As he rounded the corner of the desk, Cara begged her feet to remain firmly planted on the carpeting. With all her heart she wanted to turn and run as Julian stalked toward her. Cara gulped in trepidation, then closed her eyes to block out the bulk of the angry man. Despite her terror, she refused to back away, unconsciously squaring her shoulders as if ready to sustain a blow.

Julian had to admit she had courage.

Perversely, he found her very composure a challenge. Without considering his actions, Julian's hand shot out, his fingers closing on the girl's chin. Lifting the bowed head, he looked down into the heart-shaped face of the little American. He could feel her jaw muscles jump in fear and waited until the colorless lashes lifted to expose the girl's eyes. Then, with an expression of supreme disinterest, which he was far from feeling, Julian's eyes scrutinized her face, then let his eyes drop to roam at will over her body.

Heat washed up into Cara's face at the insulting examination. She wanted desperately to cover her chest as Julian's eyes skimmed across her bosom, seeming to probe for the figure beneath her dress. Gritting her teeth, she willed herself to stand quietly beneath his inspection.

The absolute stillness of the girl broke through Julian's rancor, and in self-disgust he whirled away, marching to the windows, to stare out blindly at the garden.

Cara shuddered in relief at the absence of the man's oppressive nearness. She was puzzled at her own reactions, which hovered somewhere between fear and excitement. Glancing up, her eyes searched the brooding figure framed in the mullioned windows.

He was undeniably handsome, Cara noted with a quickening of her pulse. A heavy thatch of black hair was cut fashionably short, curling slightly around his neck and across his forehead.

Tracing the lines of Wilton's face, Cara tried to view the disconcerting man objectively. His features were clearcut. A high forehead, over jutting black eyebrows, dominated the upper part of his face. The left brow was cut through by a jagged scar that gave his face a look of perpetual sardonic amusement. His nose was straight and his mouth full-lipped, hinting at a barely controlled sensual nature. His chin was sharply square, indicating stubbornness and determination. His eyes were hidden behind heavy lids, but Cara had no trouble recalling their piercing regard. Unable to bear the continued silence, Cara plunged into speech.

"Besides their lessons, what other responsibilities will I have with the children?"

Julian laughed shortly at the persistence of the girl. Not only had he failed to intimidate her but now she was interrogating him. It crossed his mind that Americans were, by and large, a troublesome lot. Their independent way of life had definitely undermined the working class. Unhappily, he remembered that his own wife was an American. Perhaps this is just a foretaste of my dealings with my new bride. Julian shuddered. On that uncomfortable thought, his brow furrowed, and he sank back down into the leather chair behind his desk.

Damnation, Julian thought in frustration. Granted the duchess had sent the girl and it would be a diplomatic move to hire her, it was still on the tip of his tongue to dismiss her out of hand. His instincts warred with his wish to accommodate his unseen bride, and he debated his decision concerning the governess. Shrugging impatiently, he briefly outlined Cara's duties. When he finished, there was silence, each of the antagonists considering the other.

"I will be solely responsible for them?" Cara questioned in order to clarify things in her own mind.

"For their every breath, Miss Farraday."

Cara ignored the heavily laced sarcasm in Julian's reply, asking sweetly in her turn, "And the salary, my lord?"

Julian mentioned a figure and watched as the girl tilted her head, then after a slight hesitation, nodded in decision.

"I will take the position, my lord."

Julian was dumbfounded by the audacity of the girl. She accepted as though she were conferring a favor on him. Finally the humor of the situation broke through his irritation, and laughing, he stood up facing the cheeky child.

20

"Thank you, Miss Farraday," Julian replied, making a mocking leg.

Before Cara could open her mouth to vent her anger, Julian strode to the door. Throwing it open, he summoned the hovering footman.

"Travis, take Miss Farraday to the children's wing and ask Mrs. Clayton if she would attend her there."

Cara's mouth snapped shut. Thus summarily dismissed, she whirled to follow the departing footman.

Chuckling in amusement, Julian returned to his desk. His verbal duel with the little mouse had been a welcome break in the otherwise humdrum daily grind of running the estate. Miss Farraday, despite appearances to the contrary, might be a lively addition to his household. Having met many Americans, Julian was aware that the women as well as the men prided themselves on their independence. Beneath Miss Farraday's whey-faced exterior there was a glimmer of a fiery temperament. No matter her youth, at least the children would be properly chaperoned. His hiring of the little American might be an interesting experiment. She would certainly bear watching.

Cara would have been terrified had she known Lord Wilton's thoughts. As it was, she trudged valiantly after the footman through endless corridors until, slightly out of breath, she found herself in the upper story of the children's wing. Opening a door, the liveried servant informed her that Mrs. Clayton would be with her shortly.

The bedroom was larger than Cara had expected. All the furnishings were old but buffed to a fine, satiny patina. Soft summer sunlight filtered through the dainty floral curtains, drawing her to the windows.

The view outside was breathtaking. A patchwork of greens of every shade met her eyes as she scanned the landscape laid out before her.

Weathersfield Hall was U-shaped, with her room at the top inside corner of the U. An enormous stone terrace spanned the entire base of the building. Down several shallow steps, a formal garden was laid out, and beyond that a lake glinted through the heavily treed landscape. There were wilder woods to be seen on all sides, and through the trees she could see other buildings that she assumed to be stables and other more practical buildings for the actual function of a working estate.

Feeling more oriented, Cara sat on the window seat thinking over her arrival.

She had come to Weathersfield Hall hoping to find her husband presentable and admirable. Well, he was presentable, she admitted grudgingly, with looks handsome enough for the Devil himself. However, never had she met anyone who was more arrogant, rude, and probably debauched, she added, recalling the lustful way his eyes had caressed her body. He was domineering, frightening, and obviously a bully, Cara continued, mentally listing his faults. She would never be happy married to such a man. She moaned in despair.

Unconsciously Cara clenched her hands as she recalled the interview. Perhaps she had come with too many expectations, but Julian's rude interrogation had immediately antagonized her. She had almost told him exactly how she viewed his autocratic attitude. Had it not been for the footman's timely arrival, she would have disgraced herself and her grandmother by speaking to Julian in a manner wholly unlike a governess. Cara's knees felt weak as she remembered her near disaster.

I'll just have to mind my tongue, Cara promised. Although, with a sinking heart, she realized that it would not be easy for her to accept the role of a compliant servant.

At the sound of scratching, Cara hurried to open the door. She admitted a tall, buxom woman who peered at her through sharp brown eyes. Next to this bustling dynamo, Cara felt like a recalcitrant schoolgirl.

"Lord love ya, miss, you're really not much bigger than

the children,'' the woman said, echoing Cara's own thoughts. "Well, it can't be helped," she continued briskly. "I'm Mrs. Clayton, Lord Wilton's housekeeper."

Cara curtsied and made her addresses. "I'm still a bit overwhelmed by my surroundings."

"It is a bit startling at first," Mrs. Clayton replied kindly. "I understand you are from the Americas, so I can imagine everything is quite different."

"Yes, ma'am. I suppose I'll get used to it eventually, but for now I doubt if I will be able to find my way anywhere. I'm not used to such an enormous household, and I must admit I'm a bit intimidated."

Mrs. Clayton immediately took to the girl who was so ready to admit her own nervousness. The other governesses had been very proud of their positions and kept themselves haughtily apart from the rest of the staff. The last governess had given herself airs and graces where none existed. She was glad to see the last of her, Mrs. Clayton thought, pursing her lips tightly in disapproval as she recalled the unsavory circumstances preceding her dismissal. The girl before her might be young, but she did not look to be flighty, nor the kind to assume unwarranted conceits.

"Just exactly what will be expected of me, Mrs. Clayton?"

At the raised eyebrows, Cara attempted to cover her ignorance. "Lord Wilton briefly sketched out my responsibilities, but you see, Mrs. Clayton, I have never been a governess to an English family, and I would like to be prepared so that I don't make too many mistakes. I would very much appreciate any advice you can offer me," Cara finished gracefully.

Thus appealed to, Mrs. Clayton was won over totally. She liked the girl's no-nonsense quality and determined to help all she could in what she considered a difficult situation. She gave a more detailed version of Cara's duties and then took her on a tour of the children's wing.

"Each child's room adjoins his body servant's room. Master Richard has this room," she continued, pointing to a room across the carpeted hallway. "Master Richard is nine. The boy is quiet, almost withdrawn." Mrs. Clayton sighed heavily, obvious disapproval in her voice. It was apparent she would have preferred a young hellion, which was more typical of the males of the upper classes.

"Mistress Belin has this one." There was a definite wariness in Mrs. Clayton's tone as she mentioned the child. "Miss Belin is six. I'm sure after you have met the children, you will be able to adapt your programs to each of their needs. I doubt if Richard will give you any trouble."

Cara gathered from the unspoken words that Belin probably would give her a great deal of trouble.

Across from the children's apartments, Cara was shown the schoolroom. It faced the inner courtyard, and the sun barely filtered through the tiny windows that were curtained in a somber gray. The room was meticulously clean, Spartan in aspect, with none of the softer decorative touches that Cara had seen thus far. She winced, thinking of the days she would spend penned in with the children.

Cara was thoughtful as they retraced the corridor toward her own room. Mrs. Clayton opened a door in the hallway, and Cara caught her breath in pleasure when she entered.

At one end of the room there was a large stone fireplace. Cheerful blue-figured tiles surrounded the opening and lay on the hearth where it jutted into the room. A luxurious Oriental carpet covered the floor in a lively pattern of soft blues and beige. The furniture was hidden beneath Holland covers but looked comfortable rather than decorative. The best feature of the room was the wall of beveled windows that framed a vista of the woods beyond the gardens.

"What a delightful room." Cara sighed in pleasure.

"It is charming," the housekeeper remarked. "It used to be the nursery, but you may have it as your sitting room, as it is little used now."

"But why ever not? It's the perfect place for the children to work and play," Cara exclaimed with pleasure.

"Well, as you can see"—Mrs. Clayton indicated a door on the opposite wall—"it connects with your room. The other governesses did not enjoy the close proximity to the children."

"If I am to have full control over the children's activities, I would find it totally depressing to spend my time in the schoolroom. I will need this room to be prepared immediately." Oblivious of the housekeeper, Cara vigorously whisked back the covers on the furniture to peer at the objects underneath. "And a large supply of wood for the fireplace. The children ought to enjoy working in front of a roaring fire." Then, noticing the housekeeper's startled expression at Cara's autocratic manner, she softened her voice to a more wheedling tone. "Please, Mrs. Clayton, tell me that you approve."

Unable to resist the impish grin of the little American, the older woman smiled in her turn. "I think it's a perfectly splendid idea."

Cara waited while Mrs. Clayton summoned servants to freshen the room and assist in unpacking her trunk. Thanks to Lord Wilton's efficient housekeeper, Cara was soon surrounded by a great bustle of activity. Now that her rooms were being set in order, Cara was anxious to get to know her charges.

"Where are the children, Mrs. Clayton?" Cara asked.

"Outside, I suspect," the housekeeper exclaimed, throwing up her hands. "Or just roaming around inside the Hall. When there is no governess, the children are pretty much left on their own. They come in when they're hungry, but otherwise no one pays them a great deal of attention as long as they stay out of trouble."

"And Lord Wilton permits this?" Cara asked in disbelief.

"Lord Wilton is not what one would call a doting guardian.'' Disapproval was heavy in Mrs. Clayton's manner. "He is not overused to children. He leaves it to the governess to keep them in order."

"I see," Cara responded tightly. Mentally she marked another flaw in the character of her husband. Sadly she acknowledged that, so far, there appeared to be little to admire in the man. "Well, until they turn up, I suppose it would be all right if I wandered around outside?" Cara asked. "It would be nice to begin getting my bearings in this place if I am to function at all well."

"I'll send along a light lunch," Mrs. Clayton offered. "What with traveling up from London, and now so many new things to assimilate, I suspect you must be a might peckish."

With her clothes hung neatly in the wardrobe, Cara felt more at home. For the moment her curiosity over the children outweighed her nervousness at her ability to play the part of a governess. She had had few opportunities to be around small children and was not totally convinced that she would be able to handle them correctly. She was thankful she was blessed with an abundance of common sense and a sound education. Assuming that the children did not take an immediate dislike to her, she was sure they would scrape along well together. Determined to curb her impatience and explore her surroundings, she quickly finished her lunch, tucking some cookies into her pocket to eat during her walk.

Mrs. Clayton had shown Cara the staircase beside her room that would lead her directly downstairs and outside. Following these directions, Cara discovered that the outside door led to the inside corner of the U. On her right lay the formal gardens, and to her left lay the wilder woods and the outbuildings. After briefly strolling through part of the vast gardens, she managed to locate the stables and was favorably impressed with the size and quality of the operation.

Entering the yard, Cara located Glum, the venerable head groom, and introduced herself as the new governess. Although reticent at first, Glum opened up under the obvious interest of the young American. His burly chest expanded under her praise for the cleanliness of the stables and the yard. Soon Cara was puffing to keep up with his short legs as they propelled him briskly through his domain. Glum's gnarled hands stroked each horse gently, and his weathered face puckered in pleasure as he extolled the lineage and attributes of each of the animals.

"Oh, what a beauty," Cara exclaimed, her eyes running over a dainty gray. "It's been months since I've ridden anything. And I must admit that I've rarely seen as fine a set of cattle as Lord Wilton has stabled."

"His Lordship's grandfather was responsible for beginning the stud, but Lord Wilton has added considerable to the bloodstock, miss," Glum explained. "This little filly is one of the gentlest of the new lot. But she's got good heart and a stamina I'd put up against some of the top goers."

"Can she jump?"

"It's like watching the fairies at work, miss. Her feet touch down with such grace she'd ne'er jostle a babe in arms." Glum chuckled.

"That I'd like to see." Cara laughed in response.

"When you're settled in and ready, just come and see Glum. I'll seat you on nothing that will put your knowledge to shame."

Inside the Hall, Cara discovered that the work had already been completed in the night nursery. The room fairly sparkled. A fire had been laid in the fireplace, and the furniture looked inviting and cozy. Entering her own room, she was introduced to the children's maids, Agnes and Janey. They were cheerful country girls, inclined to snicker nervously but eager to impart their views on the household.

"Mrs. Clayton said as how we could do for you as well as the children, miss," the dark, buxom Janey offered.

"I appreciate your thoughtfulness," Cara replied cautiously, not wanting to get off on the wrong footing with the girls. "I've never had anyone to wait on me before. I'll feel like real gentry."

As Cara raised her nose in the air she smiled broadly at the girls, which sent them into a fit of the giggles.

"Wait until you've seen some of the ladies what come up from London with Lord Wilton," Agnes gushed. "Oh, the dresses are ever so fine and all their great jewels and glittery things."

"A house party?" Cara asked.

"Twelve of 'em, miss," the irrepressible Agnes offered. "I peeked over the balcony just afore lunch. All prinked up, and the ladies making eyes at His Lordship. Not that he'd notice, since Lady Valencia Greeley was hangin' on his arm, just like she couldn't make it all the way into the salon."

"Lady Valencia is elderly?" Cara asked hopefully.

This question set the girls off again into laughter.

"Not by half, she ain't," Janey volunteered. "A right tarted-up beauty, if you ask me. Lots of town airs. Ever so sweet when any of the gents are around, but a sly puss when they're not."

"Her abigail is done up by the end of the day, what with Her Ladyship changing her clothes four times a day and wantin' this and that fetched till the poor gel is plumb wore out." Agnes lowered her voice to a confidential tone. "I was passin' her rooms after she'd gone off to lunch, and the place was tossed all to pieces. Must have tried on ten dresses, and each one of them thrown down in a heap. And she paints," she added, delicious horror in her voice.

"Lord Wilton don't seem to mind," Janey sniffed.

"I thought His Lordship was married," Cara stated weakly.

28

"At may be so, miss," Agnes burst in, "but word in the Hall is that it was all arranged by his father. I hear she's a proper quiz. Comes from America, which is full of rough, brutish men and frumpy women."

Seeing Cara's startled expression, Agnes remembered the new governess was an American and clapped a hand over her mouth, rolling her eyes in embarrassment. Janey clutched her apron as she would a lifeline, her face mirroring the younger girl's discomfort.

"I'm ever so sorry, miss," Agnes stuttered.

"Never mind," Cara answered kindly. "I suspect most of the people in England think the same thing." Then quickly changing the subject, she asked about the children.

"They're better off orphaned, if you don't mind my saying," Janey announced in disapproving tones. "Their mother was a flighty piece of goods, no better than she should be. Some said if the carriage accident hadn't took 'em, that their father would have been involved in an awful scandal. All set up for a duel, he was. Over some bit of muslin."

"It's lucky for the children that they've come to be with Lord Wilton," Agnes enthused. "He'll see to the right of things. A proper gentleman, His Lordship is."

"He's not setting much of an example for the children if he's carrying on with Lady Valencia." Cara could not keep the note of censure out of her voice.

"Well, gentlemen must have their pleasures, miss." Agnes, who Cara suspected was no more then fifteen, sounded for all the world like a weary matron. "He's a good man, is Lord Wilton."

"Got the Devil's own temper," claimed Janey. "Comes from gettin' his own way as a lad. But for all that, he's a fair man. He didn't used to spend much time in the country. He had his opera dancers and such in town. Lately he's been on the estate more and really takes an interest in

29

the doings. Fixed up all the tenants' cottages the last time. Better than most I could mention.''

By this time Cara had learned enough about Wilton to put her decidedly out of sorts. She had enjoyed the chatter of the girls but wanted nothing now except a wash and her dinner. Quickly she thanked the girls for their company, explaining that she would be delighted with a tray in the new schoolroom.

''Then, after the children's dinner, I would like you to bring them along to the nursery.'' At the girls' blank expressions, she questioned, ''Will they be going downstairs to Lord Wilton?''

''Oh, no, miss,'' chirped Agnes brightly. ''The children won't be seeing His Lordship. He only sees them if they need seeing.''

''I understand,'' Cara said, although she really didn't. ''Then bring them along, and tell Mrs. Clayton I would like a pot of hot chocolate and some cakes if she can manage.''

By the time that Cara had finished her own dinner, she wondered just what sort of mysterious situation existed at Weathersfield. Everyone seemed to evade her questions about the children. References were made to them, but she sensed a reticence that gave her pause. She already had enough problems coping with Wilton, but now she foresaw additional problems ahead. That there were four previous governesses did not bode well for her own success in the position.

Cara's head throbbed with an incipient headache. Wearily she rested against the soft cushions of the sofa, waiting for the arrival of the children. It had been an extremely long day. The excitement of her departure from her grandmother's had worn off after the exhausting carriage ride and then her disastrous interview with Wilton. She was unwilling to admit that her dejection had any relationship to some of the things she had heard about her husband.

Despite the fact that Cara claimed total antipathy toward Julian, she was surprised at her reaction to his apparent unfaithfulness. His affair must be fairly blatant if it was common gossip among the servants. She had never really considered the fact that he had not been eager for the marriage. Perhaps he, too, had fought against the arrangement. He might be in love with Lady Valencia and had wanted to keep himself free to marry the woman. Then, of course, his father, like Cara's, had forced him into an unwanted alliance.

Remembering her impression of Wilton's arrogance, it was inconceivable to Cara that Julian could ever be forced to do anything against his will. "I knew he was debauched," she muttered self-righteously.

At the sound of voices in the hall, Cara sprang to her feet, brushing out the wrinkles in her skirt. Her heart pounded nervously as she waited to meet the children. At her own faintheartedness she stamped her foot impatiently. After all, they were only children. This part of her masquerade should be easy, she reasoned naively.

Chapter Three

Cara bit her lower lip nervously. She knew how crucial this first meeting with the children would be. If they liked her, the month would pass quickly. However, if the children preferred, they could make her time at Weathersfield quite unpleasant.

The new schoolroom glowed in the flickering candlelight, and a fire crackled in the otherwise silent room. Comfortable chairs were circled in front of the hearth. An overstuffed sofa, patterned in a cheerful Scottish plaid, was pulled up to a low table set with a mouth-watering assortment of cakes and pastries. The sweet smell of hot chocolate pervaded the air.

The door opened on a slight, sullen-faced boy.

Despite the frown, which Cara suspected was his habitual expression, Richard Weathersfield was a handsome boy. His light brown hair was cut in the Brutus style, curling riotously despite the pomade that had been used to keep it in place. He was dressed in a dark brown velvet jacket, cut in the same fashion as his guardian's. His cravat was simpler, but the material was just as expensive as Wilton's had been. At least, Cara thought grudgingly, Julian did not appear to stint on the children's expenses. Under the gaze of steady blue eyes, Cara waited passively as the boy conducted his own scrutiny.

"I don't like governesses," Richard announced.

"That shows that you're growing up," Cara stated matter-of-factly. "I always hated mine."

"Did you really?" Then, before Cara could frame an answer, he continued in an aggrieved tone. "Actually I don't much like anything. Everything's frightfully boring."

With a graceful nod, Cara hid her amusement at his world-weary attitude. "I suppose it wouldn't be boring for a very young child. But now that you're nine, you probably find you are bored by things that used to interest you."

The boy was torn between his customary frown and a look of curiosity. Unfortunately, the scowl won out, leaving his face petulant and his carriage slouched.

Before she could comment further, the door was thrown open and Agnes, the maid, appeared, literally dragging by the neck of her dress what Cara could only assume was Belin.

Tangled black curls covered the child's head and shoulders. Curls that had not seen a brush, let alone water, for many days, hung limply down her back. Her dress was torn and streaked with dirt. Her scrawny arms and hands were smudged and scratched. Not ungently, Agnes deposited the girl on the rug in front of Cara and then beat a hasty retreat.

Looking down at the child, Cara flinched slightly at the wide brown eyes that so closely resembled Lord Wilton's. She schooled her features into peaceful lines and tried not to wrinkle her nose with distaste at the child. Catching a glimmer of Belin's expression through her tangled hair, Cara's mouth widened into a grin.

"My stars, Belin. You must turn this entire household upside down." Cara chuckled with genuine amusement.

"Don't you laugh at me, or I'll put a spell on you," the child snarled.

33

"I wouldn't waste your time, Belin. It wouldn't work on me, anyway."

"Why not?" the girl asked belligerently.

"You see, I wasn't born in England. And I don't think any of your spells would work on someone from America." Cara leaned forward in unconcern and poured out three cups of chocolate. Richard accepted his cup with a smile tugging at the corners of his mouth that was returned by Cara. "Now, Belin, since it is my first night here, I will excuse a little dirt. But tomorrow, if you wish chocolate or pastries, I expect clean hands."

Then, before the startled child could form a retort, Cara handed her a cup of chocolate and commenced to tell the two wide-eyed children about her ship's voyage to England. Perhaps the storms and adventures were more violent than had actually occurred, but there was no one to contradict her. By the time the pot of chocolate was empty and the plate of cakes bore nothing but crumbs, Cara had given the children the idea that she had many more stories to tell. Briskly she handed them into the care of the servants. With a sigh of relief, Cara sank to the carpet in front of the fireplace.

Staring into the dying flames, Cara realized she had only made a start with the children. The sullen Richard, at nine, was caught in the painful early stages of manhood. His breeding was evident in his perfect manners and intelligent, though stilted, conversation. He did not appear to be shy but was bottling some unnamed tension. Cara thought she would enjoy challenging Richard with new experiences until he released whatever emotions he had sealed away.

It was Belin who was the puzzle.

In her mind's eye Cara could recall the sad brown eyes in the dirty face. Something was tearing the six-year-old apart, so that she lashed out in anger. Although her behavior appeared highly undisciplined, there was a certain quality of intelligent planning that showed in her mannerisms. What catastrophe had befallen the child that she was in such a state of rebellion? Cara doubted that it was the death of the children's parents. From the servants' gossip, the children had seldom been in their parents' company. Like most upper class children, Belin and Richard had spent their time predominantly with governesses and others on the estate.

"How could Wilton have let this happen?" Cara fumed aloud.

The flames expanded to new life as a current of air circulated in the room from the opening door. Cara's breath caught in her throat as she stared at the shadowy figure framed in the doorway. For a moment she thought that she had merely conjured an image of her husband, and she blinked her eyes to dispel the vision.

"Good evening, Miss Farraday."

Julian's deep voice sent a shiver along Cara's spine, breaking the almost magical spell that had held her in thrall. She scrambled awkwardly to her feet, standing rigidly with her back to the fire. As she stood tongue-tied, feeling graceless and childlike, anger suffused her at her inability to appear poised in the presence of her husband.

"G-good evening, Lord Wilton," she finally stammered.

"I see that I have missed the children." Julian nodded toward the tray of dirty dishes. "Must have tarried too long over my brandy."

Warily Cara noted the snifter in Julian's hand and wondered just how much the man had drunk. Although his movements as he approached the fire were well coordinated and his speech was not slurred, Cara straightened her back, preparing to deal briskly with the man if, in fact, he were foxed.

"I'm sorry but the children have already retired, Lord

Wilton. Perhaps another evening," Cara offered, hinting for the man to leave.

"The room looks well," Julian said, waving the snifter to indicate his approval. "I doubt if I've been up here since I was a babe."

"It's a lovely room." Cara spoke warmly, then blushed as Wilton's eyes swung around to her. She was infuriated at her own reaction to Julian's presence. Staring miserably at the toes of her boots, she cursed her lack of backbone.

The silence was broken by the sounds of Julian's steps as he strolled around the room. As he neared the windows, Cara dared to peek at him through her lashes. Framed by the sparkling panes of glass, the somber black evening clothes gave him the look of a silhouette. But there was nothing insubstantial about the man. Taut muscles rippled beneath the velvet jacket lying across his shoulders. Cara's eyes fell to the trim waist, and then as they slid down the length of his thighs, she blushed in confusion. Her heart hammered in her breast, and she experienced a strange breathless quality as her eyes roamed over the figure of her husband.

Damn the man, Cara cursed silently. Why did he affect her the way he did? She tried to muster up some anger to counteract the helpless confusion she felt. Aloud she said, "Is there something you wanted, Your Lordship?"

Slowly Wilton turned away from the darkened windows, his gaze going to the girl beside the fire. In silence he took in the too-big wool dress that was at least three years out of date. The voluminous headdress he dismissed with a sneer, but the white face beneath the wimple was studied with care. Why have I come here? Julian asked himself in puzzlement. What was there about the girl that had drawn him to the schoolroom?

"I just wanted to be sure that you had been settled properly, Miss Farraday," Julian improvised.

Cara's eyelids flickered in disbelief, but there was no sign on her expressionless face that she thought his actions were unusual. "Mrs. Clayton has been all that is helpful. I had a chance to wander around, and Weathersfield is an impressive estate. The gardens are beautiful, and my rooms are charming."

"And do you find the children charming, too?"

Cara took a deep breath, opening her mouth to speak, but under the sardonic gaze of her husband, she was unable to continue. For fully five seconds her mouth hung open; then, in exasperation, she snapped it shut and hung her head in dismay.

"Come, come, Miss Farraday," Julian drawled. "Such reticence from an outspoken American. I would never have suspected you could behave so circumspectly."

"Why does Richard still have a maid instead of a man-servant?"

The words burst forth, surprising Cara as much as they startled Julian. She had so many questions about the children and was not even aware that Richard's bodyservant was one of them.

"What?" Julian barked.

"The boy is nine, Lord Wilton. He's no longer a baby to have a young girl fussing about him."

"Has the halfling complained?"

"No, sir, but I have met Janey. She's a good country girl who chatters away and, I suspect, treats him like an idiot younger brother." Cara felt the hot flush rising to her cheeks under Wilton's probing eyes, and she faltered to an end. "I—I think he should have a man to do for him."

"Anything else in my household you would change?"

"N-no, Your Lordship," Cara muttered cravenly.

Eyes glued miserably to the pattern of the rug, Cara missed the amusement that flashed across Julian's face as he made his way to the door. It was only hearing the soft click of the closing door that made her aware that she was alone again. Her cheeks blew out as she expelled the breath that she had been unconsciously holding in expectation of a setdown. "What a coward I am," Cara muttered in annoyance. "Why didn't I ask him about the children? Why didn't I find out what is wrong with Belin?" She castigated herself all the time she prepared for bed, then crawled miserably beneath the covers, only to lie awake late into the night.

In the morning Cara had breakfast with the children in the nursery. Although Belin was in a clean dress and her hair was pulled back and tied with a ribbon, she was still far from clean. She fidgeted continually during the meal, snatching food with quick, jerky movements. Whenever she caught Cara watching her, the child refused to eat, sitting rigidly with her hands in her lap. Richard ate glumly, his face cast in an unappealing expression of discontent. Despite the leaden feeling in her heart, Cara approached the day with a determined cheerfulness.

"Today we shall not have lessons," she announced brightly. "Since I am new here, I have to learn my way around. I know that you both could show me all the important places. As you are the oldest, Richard, you may lead for today."

The sullen expression lifted from the boy's face, and Cara wondered if part of Richard's problem was simply that no one paid him any attention. All boys liked to show off their knowledge, and if there was no one to impress, it might indeed make him sulky and taciturn.

"If I can't lead, I won't go," Belin screamed.

"You may suit yourself, Belin." Cara sighed. "However if you do not go with us, you will have to remain in your room until we return. Now that you have a governess again, it is time you learned to follow some rules."

Sad brown eyes lifted, and Cara flinched inwardly at the

searing pain they reflected. She noted all the signs of impending rebellion as Belin's chin jutted mutinously forward. In a moment Cara knew she would be involved in a full-blown battle of wills she was far from certain she could win.

"I really wish you would come with us, Belin," Cara ventured in her most coaxing manner. "I forgot last night to tell you about the cat that we had on board ship. I thought if we found a good spot to rest, I could tell you about her and, of course, the kittens. In fact, you could pick out a different spot to eat the lunch that Mrs. Clayton has made for us."

Belin brightened at the idea and agreed to accompany them.

By the end of the morning they had covered a great deal of ground. Cara felt a little like Scheherazade, spinning endless tales whenever there was a sign of restlessness in either of the children. On the edge of the lake she sat and told them the promised story of the cat and the kittens. It was a tale full of near disasters she made up out of whole cloth. The stories kept the recalcitrant Belin at her side, eager for more. Even Richard left behind his usual bored expression, hearing the exciting adventures in a new land. However, it was the Indian accounts, complete with battles and narrow escapes, that captured his total fascination.

"Can't we pretend we're Indians, Miss Farraday?" Belin pleaded.

"Of course, we can." Cara laughed, pleased that she had managed to stimulate their imaginations.

"We'll need some feathers and some axes and some arrows," Richard said, intent on a realistic enactment of mayhem. "Come on, Belin. I know just where to look."

Cara watched as the children raced back and forth in the woods looking for anything that could be considered a possible weapon. With a final whoop of triumph, Richard raced to Cara's side, proudly displaying two rather woebegone feathers.

"Well done, Richard," Cara praised the flush-faced boy.

"What will we use for paint?" Belin wailed.

"I think we could probably play without war paint," Cara suggested judiciously. The downcast faces forced her to reconsider. Remembering her own joyful games, she grinned in triumph. Briskly she issued instructions. While the children gathered red berries from the nearby bushes, Cara rummaged in the empty lunch basket for a dish.

"First you mash the berries up a bit." She demonstrated with a stick and then let an eager Belin take over the task. "Watch your clothes. I suspect that concoction will stain."

While Richard cheerfully set to work constructing a bevy of makeshift weapons, Cara tore a band of material from the bottom of her petticoat to fashion two headbands. The feathers were a little bedraggled, but it was obvious that the children would not care. Checking the soggy mess Belin was pulverizing, Cara announced that the war paint was ready. Using a corner of a napkin, she painted garish symbols on the children's ecstatic faces. After tying on the headbands, Cara stood back to survey her work.

"Well, you certainly look like proper little savages," Cara pronounced, inspecting their ferocious expressions.

"I'll paint you, Miss Farraday," Richard offered.

"I thought I might just be a settler."

Cara was unsure of her role as a governess, but she was positive that running through the woods with a painted face would not be considered wholly dignified.

"Please, Miss Farraday? It would be much more fun if you were an Indian, too," Belin pleaded.

"I suppose I could be a squaw, but they don't wear paint," Cara explained. However, after one look at the

40

crestfallen faces, she relented. "Unless of course it happens to be during the harvest festival."

Both children nodded solemnly.

"I was afraid of that." She laughed as the children dissolved in giggles. "In that case, the squaws would have a streak of paint right down their noses. Like this."

Gingerly Cara drew the red-soaked napkin from her forehead down to the tip of her nose. Wide-eyed with pleasure the children covered their mouths to muffle their laughter.

"Never mind, you little beasts. I think I make a charming squaw," Cara intoned seriously, then grinned as the children collapsed in glee.

"I'd say you look all the crack," Richard acknowledged when he could control his laughter. "Absolutely smashing!"

After parceling out the various crude weapons, the garish threesome split up to stalk buffalo and settlers. Richard was more enthusiastic in the pursuit of settlers, on the theory that his chances of a good fight were better. There was much shrieking and whooping as each of the Indians battled with the elements, imaginary enemies, and occasionally with each other. The game finally resolved itself into hide-and-seek.

Hurrying along the trail, Cara mopped at the perspiration dotting her upper lip. Readjusting her headdress she cursed the profusion of material, wishing she might abandon her disguise and let her hair flow freely in the warm June sunshine. She searched the woods for a possible hiding place. Nothing suited, and she walked farther along the path. Hearing the rustling of someone moving behind her, she threw herself behind the nearest bushes hoping to evade detection. The footsteps came closer, hesitated, then walked directly toward her hiding place.

Cautiously parting the greenery, Cara gasped at the sight of two polished Hessians planted solidly on the dusty path.

With a groan of pure embarrassment, Cara's eyes slid up the boots to the muscular thighs encased in buckskin breeches. She licked her dry mouth, tasting the salty perspiration on her upper lip, and her eyes traversed the trim waist and expanse of chest in the many-pocketed hunting jacket. Her glance faltered at the granite-hard chin, but as if to punish herself, she completed the survey of Julian's expressionless face and ruffled black hair.

"Are you hurt, Miss Farraday?" Lord Wilton inquired in a deep voice that sent a shiver along Cara's nerve endings.

"Thank you, my lord, but I'm perfectly all right."

Cara ground out her answer, her eyes closing in agony. Praying that Julian would walk on or, more properly, vanish off the face of the earth, she pressed her burning cheeks against the cool grass. When Cara continued to lay inert on the ground, the boots shifted restlessly.

"Are you planning to remain there for long, Miss Farraday?"

"For the rest of my life." Cara cursed under her breath. Then realizing the futility of the situation, she sighed in defeat and answered, "No, Your Lordship."

Summoning what dignity she could, she stumbled awkwardly to her feet. It took all her determination to face her husband with a look of disdain, which was somewhat marred by the streak of war paint on her face.

"You're injured!" Julian stepped forward in concern. "What happened?"

"Indians," Cara declared straight-facedly.

"I saw Richard and Belin a little while ago." Julian chuckled. "I thought their war paint was fearsome, but I didn't realize that you were a member of their tribe."

Taking Cara's arm, Julian turned her toward the light so that he could get a better look at the artistically painted face turned up to him. He had to admire the girl's coolness in such an awkward situation. Except for the flush on her

42

cheeks, she appeared totally unconcerned as he scanned her features.

He noted the clean, fresh quality of her skin and the soft brown hair of her lashes and brows. Throwing a look of disgust at the voluminous scarf on her head, he wondered idly if her hair matched her brows. His nostrils flared at the soft, flowery scent that wafted up from her tiny figure. Though the girl neither cringed nor struggled in his grasp, he felt her physical withdrawal in her very stillness. Excited by the feel of her skin, Julian drew her closer.

"The war paint is very becoming, Miss Farraday," Julian breathed hoarsely.

Stunned by the sensual quality of his voice, Cara's eyes widened in consternation.

Once again Julian was caught by the jeweled eyes that stared up at him. Beneath his hand he could feel her body quiver. It reminded him of an injured sparrow he had once held in his hand. Julian was puzzled and dismayed at his reaction to the little governess. At thirty he was long past the easily aroused passions of a callow youth. Yet, as he held the arm of the petite American, he had an overwhelming desire to kiss the luscious mouth of the little innocent. Within those blue-green eyes he sensed a sleeping sensuality that he was curious to awaken. The urge to reach up his hand to soothe the girl-child's fear, was irresistible. Unable to stop himself he stroked the back of his hand across her cheek, hearing her indrawn gasp at the contact.

A low moan issued from Cara at the flamelike contact of Julian's hand. Her senses expanded, and her arm burned where his fingers grasped her. Julian's male scent surrounded her, and dreamily she leaned into his embrace. Her eyelashes fluttered like butterfly wings as Julian's mouth closed over her trembling lips.

Julian's kiss jolted Cara like a bolt of lightning. His soft, warm lips molded to hers. At the touch of his tongue along the outer edges, her mouth opened slightly, and her senses reeled as the tip slid between her lips. Cara was awash in erotic sensations as Julian's tongue probed the soft, cushiony interior, lightly flicking her own tongue, which was rigid with an unnamed desire. Knees buckling, she lay against his chest absorbed in the sensuality of his caress.

It was the knowledge that this man was her husband that finally broke through the spell that Julian had woven. In horror she realized that Julian's actions were those of an adulterer. He did not know that he was kissing his wife. In his mind, Cara was merely the governess. An employee to be treated as a plaything, an object of his desires. As anger welled up inside her, Cara instinctively drew back her hand and slapped Julian's face.

The sound was as loud as a shot and just as startling.

At the blow Julian's head snapped back and his eyes, glazed with desire, changed to a hard brown. Disgust at his own lack of control gave his face a look of contempt as he glared down at the furious girl. As quickly as his emotions were revealed, a mask of indifference crossed his face, and he stood back, bowing mockingly to the girl.

"Your pardon, Miss Farraday," Julian drawled. "I would say I was sorry, but I fear I quite enjoyed the kiss."

"I find your behavior both insulting and depraved."

"Softly, my dear child. It was nothing."

Cara was stunned that the kiss, which had been so all-consuming for her, could be dismissed so easily. She ducked her head to hide the film of tears which threatened to overflow.

"You are a married man, Lord Wilton," Cara accused.

"So far, only in name, Miss Farraday. As I am sure you are aware, a man has certain, shall we say, urges."

Anger at his own behavior made Julian strike out at the girl. Watching her face whiten at his cruel words, he felt a momentary pang of regret. However, it would not do to

44

become involved with the little governess. Staring at the girl under lowered brows, Julian could not imagine what had possessed him. Her downcast eyes effectively dimmed the vitality of the American, and he was struck by the demure innocence that was quite outside his usual philandering. The virginal look of the girl should discourage any further approach, Julian admitted sanguinely, after all, the debauching of schoolroom chits was definitely not in his style.

"Look, Miss Farraday. It's Pennyfeather!"

At Richard's triumphant shout, Julian snorted in disgust. With a cool nod of his head, Lord Wilton spun on his heel and stalked off along the path.

It was a full moment before Cara could take in Julian's abrupt departure. Her body shook with the fury of emotions unleased by the confrontation with her husband. Hearing the shouting of her returning warriors, Cara tried to pull herself together, her mind still presenting scathing remarks she should have made to Julian. As the children approached, she brushed at the leaves and grass on her skirts.

"This is Miss Farraday, our new governess," Belin lisped.

"And this is Pennyfeather," Richard announced proudly.

Cara had been deluged during the day with the exploits of the children's friend. It was suspected that he might have been either a pirate or, at the least, a smuggler. Cara was amused that either occupation held high favor in the children's eyes. Although she wanted to make a good impression for the children's sake, Cara felt less than adequate with war paint on her face and her wits scattered by Julian's assault.

"The children have been telling me of your many adventures, Pennyfeather." Cara smiled hesitantly into the crinkly gray eyes of what she hoped was a benevolent giant.

Great hamlike hands snatched off the tweed cap perched on a thatch of frizzy hair. The hair was neither

45

brown nor white. It looked as though Pennyfeather's whole head had been spattered with white paint. As the sausage-shaped fingers kneaded the cap, his keen eyes inspected the girl, instantly discerning her agitation. The wild hairs sprouting from his eyebrows lowered over narrowed eyes as he squinted toward the Hall and Julian's departing figure.

"Found your Indians stalkin' a couple squirrels."

The children attempted a shamefaced expression but fell short of the mark. They capered around the big man who was as undisturbed as a cow might be by buzzing flies. With an economy of words, Pennyfeather dispatched them to the stream for some water, giving the distraught girl a chance to collect her scattered poise. Without impatience, he waited in silence until they returned with a dampened cloth.

"Give over," Pennyfeather ordered, holding out an enormous hand.

"Aw, Pennyfeather, only babies get their faces washed," Richard muttered as the wet cloth descended on his face.

"Quit your bleatin', young sir, and let me finish."

In fascination, Cara watched as Pennyfeather scrubbed the paint off each of the children's faces. His features screwed up in concentration, he bent to the task in total absorption. Although the children wriggled in his grasp, it was obvious that the huge man's touch was gentle. Without pausing, Pennyfeather turned to Cara, tipped her face upward and proceeded to wash the paint from her forehead and nose. Although Cara was surprised that he treated her like just one more child, she was content for the moment with her role. Surveying the three shining faces, the old man shoved the red-stained cloth into one of the pockets of his jacket and started off along the path.

Hurrying to keep up with Pennyfeather's rolling gait, Cara was pleased to find that her ragged emotions were once more under control. She refused to think about Julian for the time being. Soon she was caught by the outdoorsman's knowledge of plants and animals as he kept Richard and Belin searching for objects of interest. The silence between the two adults was comfortable with little need of words. From time to time the children squealed for attention, and then Cara and the old woodsman would admire each discovery. It amazed her that despite his heaviness, Pennyfeather's enormous boots trod silently on the paths, barely ruffling the leaves.

"You'll have to watch Pennyfeather," Cara suggested to the children. "Then you can move through the woods like shadows."

"Pennyfeather's a poacher," Richard confided in awe. "He's so quiet he can sneak up on the deer and pet them."

Apprehensively Cara glanced sideways to encounter the discomfitted grin of her companion. She hoped the boy was exaggerating because she knew that in England the punishments meted out for poaching were still harsh. From Richard's chatter Cara was aware that Julian had gamekeepers always on the alert for trespassers.

As the late afternoon sun began to glow with a reddish hue, the children were rounded up for a return to the Hall. Standing beside Pennyfeather's enormous silent figure, Cara watched Belin twirling in the sunshine.

"What's the matter with Belin?" she blurted out. During her short acquaintance with Pennyfeather, Cara had detected the giant's devotion to the children. It seemed right that she ask him how to solve the puzzle of the wild child.

" 'Tis not mine to tell," Pennyfeather's deep voice rumbled. It was not spoken unkindly.

"Will I be able to help her?"

The silent man towered over Cara's diminutive figure. Unlike her reaction to Julian, she found nothing threatening in the man's presence. Cara met his inspection calmly. Shaggy brows knitted over deep-set eyes, the old man frowned down at the young governess. His glance was neither insulting nor impertinent. The pleated headdress covering her hair caused his eyes to crinkle in merriment. After a thorough scrutiny, Pennyfeather nodded his head, indicating his approval.

"If anyone can help the lass, I think you can."

Pennyfeather's heartening words rang in Cara's ears on the trip back to the Hall. However, that evening, as she waited for the children's arrival, her heart was heavy with trepidation.

Chapter Four

The schoolroom door opened and Richard entered. At his well-groomed appearance yet closed-in expression, Cara sighed. Gone was the boy, painted face aglow, who had leapt out of a tree brandishing an Indian tomahawk.

"Richard, could you do me a favor?" Cara asked.

"I suppose so," he answered, far from enthusiastically.

"Despite the fact that the days are warm, it does get a bit cool once the sun goes down. I thought perhaps you could take care of the fire each evening. I can do it, but I thought you should be in charge. Belin might be able to help, but she is still very young."

"Oh, rather," the boy drawled, trying to hide his elation. He reached eagerly for the largest log and began to drag it over to the fireplace.

"Would you like me to show you how an Indian makes a fire?" Cara asked diplomatically.

"Oh, rather!"

Kneeling down in front of the fireplace, Cara told him how to lay the fire, starting with kindling and building up to the larger logs. Soon Richard's coat was off, and he was busily immersed in his project. Returning to her chair, Cara noticed that Belin had entered, standing woodenly just inside the doorway, her hands behind her back.

"Oh, Belin, I'm glad you've come to join us." Cara

kept her voice carefully cheerful, although her heart sank at the sight of the filthy child. As on the night before, her dress was streaked and her hair tangled. Preparing herself for the fight to come, Cara sank warily onto the edge of the sofa cushion. "You'll have to come over here if you want to hear the story. Richard's working on a fire for us, so everything will be nice and cozy."

Rigidly the child approached, until she stood directly in front of Cara. There were traces of tears on her cheeks and an inconsolable sadness in the brown eyes that shrank before Cara's glance. Slowly Belin withdrew her hands from behind her back and placed them in Cara's lap, then closed her eyes waiting in agony for the inspection. As she looked down at the hands in her lap, Cara understood the root of Belin's rebellion

Between each pudgy finger of both hands there was a tiny webbing of skin.

Pity made her automatically reach out to Belin, but she dropped her hands before she touched the child. Angrily Cara wondered why no one had told her about the slight deformity. It explained so much of the child's behavior. Schooling her voice to its most matter-of-fact tone, she picked up the tiny cold hands in her own warm ones.

"Why, they're perfectly clean, Belin." She had to smile. Belin had taken Cara at her word and had washed her hands in order to participate in the treats. But only her hands. From the wrists up, water had not touched her body. "Here, I'll pour you some chocolate."

The child relaxed, her body sagging in her relief that Cara hadn't mentioned her hands. Cautiously she peeked up at her governess. Her face was a complex of fear and puzzlement. The fear won. Snatching her hands away from Cara, she waved them in front of her body. Her face was screwed up in agony, her body fairly vibrating with her agitation.

"Can't you see my hands?" Her eyes were wide open, spitting fire. "I'm a witch's spawn!"

Although her heart raced in fear, Cara answered calmly, knowing how important her actions were to the furious child. "Of course I saw your hands, Belin. I thought you just didn't want me to know your secret. But even in America we've heard of the sign of the Frog Princess." Then, quickly, while the child was still off balance, Cara hurried on. "Sit down, Belin. Richard's got the fire going now, and as soon as we get some chocolate, I'll tell you about it. I'm sure you've been told the story a hundred times, but perhaps Richard hasn't heard it."

Ignoring the spluttering child, Cara busied herself handing around the chocolate and cakes. Quietly she complimented Richard on the fire. His face flushed with pride as he sipped the hot chocolate. Belin sat rigidly on the edge of her chair, clutching her cup in agony of suspense. Finally Cara reseated herself and began her story. Both children's eyes were fixed on her face.

"You see, a long, long time ago a king had a beautiful daughter who was in love with a handsome prince. He lived across a huge body of water. One day she wanted to see him, and there were no boats to take her across the water. A wicked wizard told her he would change her into a frog so that she could swim across." Cara spoke softly, noticing that although Belin was totally absorbed in the fairy tale, her body fairly simmered with tension. "Delighted with the clever plan, the princess let him turn her into a frog. In the twinkling of an eye, she swam to the other side. But the wizard had tricked her, and she did not change back into a princess. She remained a frog. The prince married someone else when he thought he had lost his true love. So, every night the Frog Princess sat on a lily pad and cried. Even today, on certain nights you can hear her cry."

51

"But what's that got to do with my hands?" Belin wailed.

"As you probably know, every hundred years a girl is born with hands like yours. It's a great honor, you know. It means that if she ever falls in love with someone across the water she won't have to turn into a frog. Her hands will help her swim."

For a moment the child sat stock-still, and then two huge tears rolled down her cheeks and her whole body shook in a shuddering cry. She dropped her cup and wrapped her arms around her knees, rocking back and forth in an agony of grief. Alarmed at the child's reaction, Cara scooped the trembling girl onto her lap and rocked and petted her, murmuring words of comfort.

Richard, who had been watching with brotherly disinterest, finally spoke. "Ghisele told Belin she was a witch's spawn and would burn in hell, no matter what she did."

"Who is Ghisele?" Cara asked, mentally condemning the woman to eternal damnation.

"She was our old nanny. I think she was a witch herself." Richard sounded more hopeful than worried. "She said that's why our mother didn't want to see Belin. It would be like looking at the Devil."

"Nonsense," Cara snapped.

"Then how come our mother never wanted to have us around?"

Belin had stopped her trembling and now lay rigid in Cara's lap.

"To be perfectly honest, Richard, I don't know. I didn't know your mother, so I can't be sure." Cara knew what she said would be very important in her future dealings with the children. She knew she needed to be honest. "There are some people that just aren't very comfortable around children. They don't know what to say to them, so they just take the easy way out and try to stay away from them."

"I never know what to say, either," Richard confided, easily accepting her explanation.

"She didn't want to see my hands. When she looked at them, she always cried," Belin accused.

Cara cursed the insensitivity of the children's mother.

"Well, Belin, if you were ashamed of your hands, perhaps she felt sorry that you were sad, and that made her cry." Cara looked down at the girl in her lap, wanting to hug away all the hurts. "I don't know, Belin. I honestly don't."

Red-rimmed eyes stared into Cara's blue-green ones. Used to ridicule and evasions, the little girl recognized the honesty of her governess's reply. Belin blinked, accepting the fact that Cara did not know the answers to some questions and, childlike, skipped to another subject.

"Does that mean I can swim?"

"No. Unless you've practice, you won't be able to swim. And by the looks of you, young lady, I don't think you've been near very much water."

"If I'm dirty, no one looks at my hands." The streaked face was wreathed in an enchanting smile, and Cara hugged her impulsively.

"So that's your game, is it?" Cara beamed at the girl whose smile transformed her. "I have a proposition for you. If you take a bath and wash your hair tomorrow, I'll teach you both to swim. Is it a bargain?"

Belin hugged Cara for an answer, and Richard whooped with delight. The remainder of the evening passed quickly with tales of princes and warriors, and other stories culled from Cara's memory of her own childhood.

After the children left for bed, Cara changed into her nightgown but found she was too restless to sleep. Annoyed, she rummaged in the wardrobe, groaning at the atrocious plaid woolen robe she found among her acquired wardrobe. Cara belted the bulky material around her waist, trying not to trip on the hem, which dragged on the floor as she walked barefoot into the schoolroom. Prodding the dying fire with a poker, Cara sighed as the flames rekindled and the heat fought off the chill of the room. Pacing to the windows she smiled at her reflection in the darkened panes. The lacy nightcap looked ludicrous with the serviceable plaid robe. Cara promised herself when she returned to her grandmother's, she would burn the offending article.

The hallway door opened, sending the flames shooting up in the fireplace. Gasping in fright, Cara swung around as Julian strode across the threshold. Clutching the robe at her throat, she pressed against the windows, her heart pounding as her husband stalked toward her. Cara closed her eyes tightly to shut out the huge figure looming in front of her. Bracing herself she waited for the assault.

"I am not here to ravish you, Miss Farraday," Julian snapped, offended by the fear on the girl's face. "I've never had a penchant for plaid."

Stiffening at the insult, Cara drew herself up and stared coldly at Julian's raised eyebrow. "One should never mock those less fortunate."

"Hah!" Julian snorted. He averted his eyes, as though unable to look at the atrocious garment.

"You shouldn't be here, Lord Wilton."

"I was passing by."

"Really, Your Lordship? Looking for the children, no doubt?"

"All right. All right. I came to apologize," Julian muttered under his breath.

Cara had to smile at his peevish tone of voice. It was obvious that her husband was unused to apologizing for his behavior. Yet, despite her gratification at his words, she still felt anger.

"When I took the position as governess, I did not suspect that I would be subjected to such insults, Lord Wilton," Cara accused.

"I assure you, Miss Farraday, that your sensibilities will

54

not be further enraged. Put it down to a touch of the sun and the uncontrolled lusts of a gentleman.''

It was Cara's turn to snort with amusement. Although Julian's apology was sarcastically phrased, she did find a sense of embarrassment behind the taunting words. Pulling herself up primly, Cara prepared to be gracious.

"I think it will be best for us to start over, Lord Wilton. The encounter in the woods never happened.''

"I have already forgotten it,'' Julian replied, his voice filled with indifference.

Cara was surprised when she felt a sharp pang of regret at his words. She chided herself, remembering that Julian's behavior was insulting at best, adulterous at worst.

"Is there anything else, Lord Wilton?''

"My man Craten recommended Barrett,'' Julian said, to Cara's total mystification.

"Recommended him for what? And who is Barrett?''

"Barrett is one of the footmen. He's just sixteen, and Craten, my valet, thought he ought to be able to take care of Richard.''

"I see,'' Cara said, finally understanding that they were talking about a servant to act as valet for Richard. "I'm glad.''

"Craten's standards are more exacting than the Regent's. He'll keep an eye on Barrett, so that by the time Richard goes through the man-milliner stage, he can keep the boy from some of the gaudier excesses of fashion.''

Julian's words filled Cara with a warm glow of gratitude. She searched her husband's face, looking for a softening of his normal autocratic expression. Her eyes were drawn to his lips, and she remembered vividly their pressure on her own mouth. Hot color rose to her cheeks, and she pulled her bathrobe protectively around her.

"What will happen to Janey?'' Cara asked, pulling her thoughts back to the discussion.

"She'll help Mrs. Clayton do, uh things." Julian airily waved his hand to indicate Janey's new duties.

"Thank you, Lord Wilton."

At the softly spoken words, Julian's head swung around to stare at the governess. He had expected a more acerbic comment and was surprised at the simple response. He winced at the garish robe, his eyes transfixed by a particularly discordant shade of orange that ran around the uneven hem. As if the girl sensed his scrutiny, she quickly tucked her bare toes modestly away from his prying eyes. The childish gesture struck Julian with the vulnerability of the girl, and he was further discomfited by his behavior in the woods. He wondered at his own presence in the schoolroom at such an hour and chastised himself for remembering the soft innocence of the young girl's lips.

"That will be all, Miss Farraday," Julian announced brusquely, spinning on his heel and stalking out of the room.

Cara stood transfixed, staring after the departing figure. Although relieved, she felt a spurt of anger at the suddenness of his departure. Grumbling and muttering over Julian's rudeness, Cara banked the fire for the night and returned to her bedroom.

Wriggling luxuriously under the covers, Cara woke slowly. She stretched her arms above her head and yawned, letting full wakefulness steal gradually through her body. She was surprised at the bright sunshine that poured in the windows, puddling in cheerful splotches on the carpet. Reaching for her watch pin on the table beside her bed, she was aghast at the lateness of the hour.

Cara leaped out of bed and hurried to the wardrobe, wondering that no one had roused her for breakfast. Making a moue of distaste, she pulled a brown merino dress out of the wardrobe. She remembered all the lovely dresses she had brought to England and moaned at the graceless dress with the prim white collar and bulky skirt. She gazed wistfully into the mirror as she tied the stiff cloth of her headdress, making sure that her hair was completely covered. I look like a poor postulant, waiting with little joy the prospect of joining the nunnery, she thought unhappily. She sighed and quickly opened the door to the nursery.

On entering the schoolroom, she was greeted by Richard, with a conspiratorial grin on his face. After a courteous greeting he stood, hands behind his back, rocking back and forth on the heels of his shiny black boots. Before Cara could do more than note his restrained eagerness, the hallway door opened and Mrs. Clayton sailed in, followed by a line of servants with loaded breakfast trays. The oak table by the windows was covered with a snowy linen cloth and sparkled with crystal and china. The housekeeper smiled broadly at Cara, then turned to face the door as though waiting for an apparition. At Richard's widening eyes, Cara swiveled to find the object of his bemusement.

Belin, sparkling clean, stood in the doorway.

Cara caught her breath in amazement, for Belin did, in fact, look like an apparition. She was exquisitely petite, tiny bones covered by creamy skin that would have been envied by the most notorious court beauty. She wore a blue-and-white sprigged muslin dress covered by a starched white apron edged with a delicate ruching of white. Her midnight-black hair was brushed to a high sheen and drawn back by a wide blue velvet ribbon, showing off her tiny shell-pink ears. But it was in her face that Cara saw the greatest difference. Her brown eyes that had held such infinite sadness were shining with happiness as she held her immaculate hands out for inspection.

"Well, Belin, so that's what you look like under all that dirt!" Cara exclaimed briskly as she walked toward her. She knelt down in front of the shining child and spoke so that no one else could hear. "Do you suppose I could give you a great big hug? It's supposed to be good luck to kiss anyone who has the sign.''

Belin hurled herself into Cara's arms with a delighted squeal. As she lifted the child, carrying her to the table in triumph, Cara noticed Mrs. Clayton dabbing self-consciously at her eyes, but she was too busy blinking to comment.

''We are a little late with breakfast,'' Mrs. Clayton explained quietly. ''Early this morning Belin demanded a bath, so I thought it would be better to hold off your meal until she was properly ready.''

Cara gathered that Belin's bath was such an unusual occurrence that Mrs. Clayton felt it called for a celebration. Over the heads of the children she smiled gratefully at the older woman, who, with an answering grin, bustled the servants out the door. Cara watched with enchantment as Belin ate her breakfast with dainty movements of her little hands. It was true that she still was slightly self-conscious about her fingers, but gone were the quick, snatching movements of the first morning. In record time the children and their governess filled themselves with ham, eggs, and freshly baked rolls, washed down by hot chocolate and a pungent orange-flavored tea.

The happy threesome hurried outside and raced down to the lake. The sun was warm in the late morning, and they wandered around the edge of the lake looking for the most likely spot for the swimming lessons. On the far side they found a small cove well covered by trees, to keep them out of sight of the Hall and the other buildings. The water appeared to be shallow, with a white sand bottom.

''I think this would be a perfect spot,'' Cara announced.

Although she would have liked to ask Mrs. Clayton about the suitability of swimming, Cara was sure the woman would be scandalized. Cara's father had taught her to swim at an early age, and she had spent many a hot afternoon in the water. However, her father had been rather progressive when it came to his daughter. He had felt that she ought to learn to ride, swim, and shoot and to be as educated as the boys she grew up with. In America, being female had been less of a handicap. In England, she suspected, Belin would be under far more restrictions. Cara felt that once the swimming lessons were an established fact, Mrs. Clayton would be less likely to frown on the activity.

Belin was divested of all but her chemise and one petticoat, although the child showed every indication of preferring to go into the water *au naturel.* Richard swam in his trousers and shirt.

For a child who had avoided water for so long, Belin took to it immediately. Richard was more hesitant, cautiously entering the water and listening attentively to Cara's instructions. After a great deal of coaxing on Cara's part, he lay across her hands and, after considerable practice, had more or less mastered the elementary stroke.

In the beginning Cara had hiked up her long skirts, but as she had become more involved, they had fallen into the water, and she was now wet to the knees. She chaffed at the restrictions of society and wished she could throw off her clothes and join the children in the water. She knew how much easier it would be for them to learn if they could see how she cut the water.

"Can't you come in, too, Miss Farraday?" Belin begged.

" 'Fraid not, dear. I doubt if it would be considered quite the thing."

Standing in the shallows, Cara wriggled her toes in the sand, delighted with her freedom from the cramping half boots she had been wearing. She watched the children, smiling at the high-pitched giggles that accompanied their efforts. Calling instructions to Richard, she was pleased at his attempts to help Belin to float. She applauded enthusiastically each of their efforts as they shouted for her to watch.

59

"I think we better call it quits for today. I don't want you to get too tired, or you won't have any energy left for tomorrow. Besides, I'm getting hungry."

Tucking up her skirts, Cara waded out to the children. She reached down to take Belin's hand, but as she touched the wet fingers, her waterlogged skirts tumbled down and the shift of weight tipped her forward. Before she could fall into the water, Cara jerked her body backward. But she had overcompensated, and with madly flailing arms, she splashed down into the cool water. Both children rushed to her aid but, realizing they were too late to help, threw themselves beside her, gasping in hysterics. Realizing the ridiculousness of her position, Cara joined in the general hilarity. Still laughing, she struggled to her feet, hugging the children to her. She staggered toward the shore, smiling broadly.

Looking up, she was speared by Lord Wilton's brown eyes.

Julian sat a deep-chested bay stallion directly above the pile of clothing on the shore. He was accompanied by another gentleman who was also mounted. Cara felt the blood rushing to her face and groaned in an agony of embarrassment.

"Good morning, Miss Farraday," drawled Lord Wilton. "Are we interrupting some more lessons?"

"Lord Wilton." Cara nodded with a composure she was far from feeling. She ground her teeth and straightened her back, trying to appear unconcerned at her disheveled appearance. With a steady pace she strode out of the water, reaching down to retrieve one of the towels she had brought along.

Trying desperately to ignore the presence of Julian and his companion, Cara handed a towel to Richard, who proceeded to dry himself sullenly as he cast angry glances at the intruders. Belin, full of enthusiasm from the exercise, was far from cowed by the presence of the adults. Chirping and chattering, she shook herself like a puppy, spraying water in every direction.

"Miss Farraday was teaching us to swim, Uncle Julian. It's ever so nice." She wriggled happily as Cara tried to dry her. "Miss Farraday says I'll be a smashing swimmer 'cause I've got a secret."

"Perhaps you'll tell it to me sometime, Belin."

Julian pushed back the black curls on his forehead with a leather-gloved hand, looking at the little girl with a puzzled expression. He watched her for a moment, then raised an eyebrow at the governess. Without words, Cara knew he was questioning the change in the child, and she nodded her head in confirmation.

"I haven't seen either of you children in quite a while. Perhaps you would care to join me and my guests tonight after dinner?"

Although the invitation was phrased as a question, his tone made it evident that it would be a command performance. In two days Cara had already had enough confrontations with Julian and wondered about the possibility of avoiding the evening's audience. She considered smallpox or typhoid, but assumed, the way her luck was running, that any dread disease would arrive too late to spare her from the coming interview. Groaning inwardly before those sparkling brown eyes, she bowed to the inevitable.

"I'm sure the children would be delighted."

With a flash of white teeth, Julian grinned at the obvious omission of the young woman's own pleasure in the audience. He had been correct in his original supposition that the addition of Miss Farraday would enliven his household. The girl certainly had a penchant for getting herself into awkward, not to say unusual, situations. Chuckling, he stared at the bedraggled group. Conscious of his companion's restive movement, he drew himself up in his saddle.

Julian had not missed the hiss of appreciation from the man beside him as the governess's slender curves were

61

revealed by the water-soaked material of her dress. He scowled blackly at the man, then shrugged his shoulders as if bowing to the inevitable. His voice, which had been teasingly sarcastic, was now formal, tinged with ice.

"Your pardon, Miss Farraday. I seem to be forgetting my manners. May I present Richard and Belin's other uncle. This is Sir Edward Tallworth. His sister was the children's mother."

Painfully aware of her drenched state, Cara barely managed a graceful curtsy. The children echoed her greeting, but she herself refused to look up at either horseman.

"Miss Farraday is the children's governess," Wilton explained. "She was hired to keep the children out of trouble." Then, noticing the gleam of appreciation in Edward's eye, he snarled, "Let's be off. We've wasted enough time with these aquatic exercises."

Belin wilted at the sudden desertion of the two men. But it was Richard's stricken expression that dismayed Cara as the boy blinked rapidly to keep back the tears. Neither gentleman had addressed the boy, and now his face held the shuttered, sullen look that Cara had begun to dread.

"Well, my dears, I certainly did land us all in the soup," Cara said briskly. "I don't suppose I look so much like a governess as a drowned rat."

"Did you see Uncle Julian's face when he saw you with water running all down your dress?" Belin chirped.

"I'm very glad I didn't, Belin. I doubt if I made a very good impression on your other uncle, either."

"Uncle Edward did look surprised. You do look a proper mess." The irrepressible child laughed as she looked up at her governess.

"What a monstrous little girl you are." Cara grinned, hugging Belin's wet body.

"I bet he won't bother you as he did our last governess," Belin continued, innocently answering one of the questions Cara had been wanting to ask. "I heard Cook say it was Uncle Edward's fault that Mademoiselle Corday went away so sudden. But I don't know why it was because of Uncle Edward. She was going to get married and get a baby. At least, that's what Janey and Agnes said.''

"That's enough, Belin," Cara interrupted the busy stream of backstairs gossip. "I don't think it's very lady-like to listen to the servants' chatter.''

"If I don't listen, then I would never know what is going on," the child answered reasonably, eyes twinkling with mischief.

Richard finished drying himself and stood silently waiting until Cara finished dressing Belin. Then, shoulders held stiffly, he trudged off in the direction of the Hall. Clutching Belin's hand, Cara hurried to catch up with him.

"Well, Richard, I guess there's nothing for it," Cara said. "We'll have to put in an appearance after dinner. We'll get all dressed up and show everyone that we really are three very well-behaved people.''

"It won't do any good," Richard snapped. "Uncle Julian still won't like me, and everyone will stare at Belin's hands," he finished brutally.

"As for Belin, everyone will be so astonished at how clean and pretty she looks, they'll forget all about her hands," Cara promised stoutly. Then, noticing the look of fear on the face of the child, she squeezed her hand and smiled to dispel the little girl's trepidation. "They'll all say she's a changed changeling.''

Belin giggled uneasily and clung a little tighter to Cara's hand.

"Besides, Richard," Cara continued, "I'm sure your Uncle Julian thinks you're a fine young man.''

"No! He hates me! He hates me!" shouted Richard, breaking into a run.

Amazed at his outburst, Cara stood still, watching as the sobbing boy disappeared into the Hall. Feeling a tug on her hand, she looked down into Belin's serious brown eyes.

"He's right, you know. Uncle Julian does hate him."

"But why, sweetheart?"

"It's because of the horses. Richard was in the carriage when the accident happened to our mother and father. He was asleep, and then he bumped his head when the horses bolted, and then he woke up, and now he won't ride horses anymore, and that's why Uncle Julian hates him," Belin finished, breathless but triumphant.

"Poor little boy," Cara said under her breath. Anger at Lord Wilton's insensitivity coursed through her body. How could the man be so lacking in compassion? What a despicable creature her husband was.

Handing Belin over to the capable hands of Agnes, Cara continued to her own room. After soaking in a hot bath and changing into a dry set of clothes, she felt better, although still angry. Thoughtfully she paced her room, then returned outside to the stables in search of the head groom, Glum. After a long and informative talk, she and the bandy-legged man devised a plan that Cara hoped might help Richard overcome his fear of horses. She was contented with her day until she remembered the ordeal scheduled for the evening.

The thought of being scrutinized by Wilton's cold eyes sent a tremor of apprehension down Cara's spine. Her grandmother had cautioned her to remain inconspicuously in the background. She doubted if the duchess would approve of her performance so far. Once more bracing her shoulders as if going into battle, Cara went indoors to prepare for the evening.

"Hold still, Belin, or I'll never get his sash tied correctly."

Cara knew her voice was unnaturally sharp, but her frayed nerves were close to breaking. The children had been dressed and brought to her for a last minute inspection before they went down to see their guardian.

"There, now. That's just perfect." Cara patted the bow in place and stood back to inspect the children one final time.

Richard was impressive, from the frothy lace of his cravat to his shiny black boots. Gowned in pink, Belin looked angelic.

"I doubt if anyone will recognize us as the group of ragamuffins we were this morning," Cara announced archly, eliciting a weak smile from Belin and a vacant stare from Richard. He wore his habitual sulky expression, and Cara knew that for him the evening would be a disaster.

Quickly turning to the mirror, she examined her own appearance. She had chosen a dark mustard-colored wool dress, bulky and uncomfortable for a June evening. The matching cowllike headdress hung limply across her shoulders and down her back. Framed by the yellowish-brown material, her naturally pale complexion held an unhealthy pallor, accentuated by the rice powder she had used to cover her brows and lashes. There was a ghostly quality to the nondescript figure in the mirror that amused Cara even as she winced at her nonpersonality. "Grandmother would approve," she muttered as she followed the children out of the room.

Outside the double doors of the large salon, Cara pressed each hand and nudged the children forward as the footmen threw open the doors. While all eyes were on Richard and Belin, Cara slid inconspicuously along the silken wall just inside the doorway.

The salon was odd-shaped, with a rounded bay jutting out toward the back gardens. It was lavishly furnished in velvets, satins, and brocades; however, despite the heavy furnishings, the room possessed an airy quality, due to myriad beveled windows that reflected the candlelight and picked up the greens and golds that predominated and refracted the color like tiny suns glowing on the perimeter. The high, vaulted ceiling was ornamented with richly carved plaster oddments and populated by glittering chandeliers hanging strategically over the bay area and a comfortable seating area.

Cara smiled, remembering her grandmother's comment that "Nobody ever looks at servants." Aside from a stir of activity as the children entered, her own presence had gone unnoticed. It was as though she were invisible, watching the players on a stage.

Her heart swelled with pride as she watched Belin chattering gaily, the only sign of nervousness a slight fidgeting with her dress sash. Richard was having a more difficult time. He stood ramrod straight, answering questions thrown at him by his uncle, Edward Tallworth, the man who had been with Julian at the lake.

"The pain was excruciating, Letitia," a heavily rouged octogenarian shouted at her equally ancient companion. "It radiated all down my right leg. It was the outside of enough that I actually had to resort to a cane."

"Well, my dear, that's what comes of all those rich foods." Letitia patted her diamond necklace, adjusting it more comfortably beneath her double chin. "It's gout, for certain."

"Nonsense!" the old woman snapped. "That's for old fogies."

"La, Harriet. It's not as if we're in our first bloom of youth." Letitia jabbed her fan into her friend's rib cage, earning herself an affronted stare. "In my mind I'm still twenty, but when I look around, I'm surprised to note all the young ones. Innocent lambs, the lot of them."

Cara smiled as both ladies raised lorgnettes to survey the assemblage. She felt slightly sinful, eavesdropping on the women's conversation. Her own eyes went to the whist players in the bay area. She carefully noted the details of the ladies' silk and muslin dresses, sighing over the beautiful jewels sparkling at exposed bosoms and wrists. The men's clothes she barely glanced at, except those of one or two of the more outrageous court dandies. Having satisfied herself as to the current fashions, her gaze wandered until it rested on Julian.

Trying to steady her rapid heartbeat as she looked at her husband, Cara had to admire the picture he made. He wore a dark blue superfine jacket with a darker-hued brocade waistcoat, unadorned by anything except a single gold watch fob. His cravat, tied in what Richard had called a waterfall, rippled down his immense chest. As he talked to the children, his head was turned full face toward Cara, and her eyes touched the fine features and brown eyes half-concealed by coal black lashes. His dark curly hair tumbled across his forehead, and he periodically brushed it back in annoyance.

"I always said her father was a want-wit. Valencia's lucky that her mother is gone. Now, there was a sharp one."

Cara's wandering attention was brought back abruptly to the older women's conversation. Valencia's name had been mentioned by Agnes and Janey, and their comments had been in no way complimentary. It took several minutes for Cara to weave together the backstairs gossip to realize the woman under discussion was the Lady Valencia Greeley, assumed by all to be her husband's current mistress.

". . . no better than she should be!" Harriet finished breathlessly. "Can't believe her father hasn't twigged to the situation."

Letitia leaned forward, her hand bracing her ample bosom as though to keep her fluttering heart within the tightly laced bodice. Lowering her voice, she spoke with relish. "I hear that their pockets are to let. But looking at Valencia, one would never suspect. That pink dress is one of Madame Chapair's creations, not some pinch-penny seamstress's as Valencia would have you believe."

Once again the lorgnettes were raised, and Cara's eyes followed to the woman seated beside Julian on the sofa.

Lady Valencia Greeley was beautiful. She was small, but her figure was quite breathtaking, from her voluptuous bosom to her curvaceous hips. Soft little hands fluttered girlishly as she plied her fan. The dress in question was of the softest shade of pink tulle, fragile as a cobweb. On another woman it would have been insipid, but Cara grudgingly admitted Valencia wore the dress with a piquant flair. A band of ruffles foamed at the low neckline, giving coy glimpses of the white flesh it was supposed to conceal. Her head was molded by waves of golden tresses swept up to the back of her head, where they cascaded in spiraling curls intertwined with pink ribbons.

". . . beauty won't last forever," continued the indefatigable Harriet. "She appears to have a dash of excess flesh under her chin. And just look at her arms! My dear, she'll be waddling in another five years," the older woman announced happily.

Through narrowed eyes Cara scrutinized Valencia, trying to be objective. She did not really consider the woman a rival for Julian's affections. At first, Cara had been disturbed by her husband's unfaithfulness, but had reminded herself that it was common enough for a married man to have a mistress. However, being sensible in the abstract, Cara found, was far different from being objective now that she was facing the actual object of Julian's desires. After all, he is my husband, she thought, eyeing the young woman carefully.

Initially, Valencia appeared to be in the first bloom of youth.

She had a heart-shaped face, with a deep widow's peak set above slanting green cat's eyes. Although the eyes were small, they were balanced by the wide sweep of brows above and the tiny pouting mouth below. A beauty patch nestled in the valley of a dimple in her cheek. Although her very appearance called out an innocence of unawakened passion, there was a sleepy awareness in the sensuality of her eyes and mouth. As Cara watched, Valencia dropped her hand to caress Julian's leg. It was but an instant's movement, and then hand and face were back to their pose of girlish innocence.

To her chagrin, angry emotion washed over Cara. Lowering her eyes to hide her fury, she felt her cheeks redden and looked up suddenly, only to be skewered on her husband's sardonic gaze.

Julian had been aware of Cara's presence since she entered the room. There was something about the girl that mystified him. She carried herself with an air that bespoke both education and breeding. Young in years, perhaps, but her face, plain at first glance, held maturity and character. He noted in amusement that Miss Farraday definitely was an innocent. She had obviously seen Valencia's caress, and Julian was delighted by the look of outrage that passed across the little governess's face.

His eyes scanned the faces in the room, stopping abruptly when he noticed Edward Tallworth's interest in the young woman. Miss Farraday was definitely not Edward's normal type; he generally gravitated toward the fluttering beauties or aging and moneyed widows. Damn the man, Julian thought. Couldn't he leave my staff alone?

"That will be all, children," Julian interrupted rudely, surprised at his own sudden burst of anger.

"But, Uncle Julian . . ." Belin began in her childish lisp. Tears trembled at the corners of her eyes as she reached out blindly for Richard's protective hand.

"Thank you, Uncle Julian," Richard commented stolidly as he made a leg to the rest of the company. "Come along, Belin."

Cara was proud of the young man who gathered Belin against his side and walked with concentrated dignity toward the door. She herself slid along the wall, escaping the salon with a sigh of relief.

69

"Well done, my dears," Cara congratulated the children. "Your behavior was exemplary."

"Is 'zemplurry' good?" Belin asked anxiously, still shaken by their abrupt dismissal.

Cara leaned down and hugged the child. "Not just good, Belin, excellent."

Belin immediately brightened, but Richard cast both females a scowl of disgust, refusing to be placated. Cara herself was relieved to be away from Julian's eyes and the devastating effect they had on her nervous system.

Chapter Five

"What will we do this morning, Miss Farraday? Can we swim again? Would you like to visit the Dorsetts' farm and see the new piglets?"

Cara listened in amusement to Belin's ebullient chatter. Even at the early breakfast hour, it was difficult to stem the child's flow of enthusiastic suggestions. Once Belin had come to terms with her own private devils, her appetite for life had redoubled.

"Mrs. Clayton has told me that you have a beautiful doll collection, Belin," Cara remarked at the end of the meal.

"Oh, yes. It's ever so fine. My father used to bring me a new one every time he came back from London. There's big ones and little ones. I must have . . . lots," she finished breathlessly.

"I would very much like to see the dolls, but I suppose you want to have time to get them ready to be presented," Cara suggested.

"Yes, it's true." Belin bit her lip, torn between impressing Miss Farraday and showing her the dolls immediately. "Some of them haven't had their hair brushed in ever such a long time."

"I have an idea, Belin. Richard and I have something to do this morning and that would give you time to get everything ready. I'm sure that Agnes would be happy to help you. Then, after lunch, I could come and be properly introduced.''

Belin turned the idea over in her mind. As Cara had hoped, the child accepted the plan and was eager to begin. The little girl left, badgering Agnes with demands for soap, water, and brushes. Cara, with an unenthusiastic Richard in tow, marched outside, heading for the stables.

Although the boy stiffened when aware of their destination, he did not refuse to accompany her.

Entering the stable yard, Cara found Glum directing two of the young boys in saddling a black Arabian stallion. Richard flinched as the stallion snorted and pawed the packed earth, but the plucky lad held his ground. The horse was beautiful, big, but sleekly muscled. A deep chest indicated he would have reserves of stamina as well as speed. Glum waited while the horse was saddled, then tipped his cap to Cara.

''Morning, Miss Farraday. Richard. Come see what we've got for ye.''

His worn boots beat a steady tattoo on the oak floors as he led the girl and the reluctant boy to the last box in the line of stalls. Looking in over the door, Cara smiled in satisfaction at the spindle-legged colt inside.

''Thank you, Glum. I think he'll do nicely.''

Doffing his cap, the old man nodded, studiously avoiding looking at the glowering boy beside the young governess. Richard had been on his way to being a fine horseman until the unfortunate accident with his parents. The head groom had talked to Miss Farraday and hoped her plan would work.

''Ye'll find everything ye need, miss,'' Glum threw over his shoulder as he stumped back to his duties.

Eyeing the warily tensed boy, Cara nervously wrung her hands. She approached Richard slowly, standing in front

72

of him in silence until he was forced to raise his eyes to her face.

"Richard, can you keep a secret?"

"Maybe."

"I'm not sure just how to explain," Cara admitted. "You see, in America I used to ride a great deal. But when my father got sick, I didn't ride for a long time. I was busy taking care of him."

"Did he die?" Richard asked bluntly, curious in spite of himself.

"Yes, he did. I felt awfully bad at the time. I suppose you remember how you felt when your own parents died?"

"I didn't feel anything," the boy snapped, hostility written all over his face.

"I know what you mean." Cara purposely misunderstood. "I was numb at first, too, but then I felt terrible. So I let a little more time go by, when I didn't ride." She paused, hoping she would see some encouragement from Richard, but his eyes were downcast, staring fixedly at the toe of his boot. "At any rate, I waited so long that now I'm afraid to ride again."

Cara held her breath as Richard's head snapped back, eyes wide, but before she could continue, all emotion was wiped from his face, and he stared at her with expressionless eyes. Cara's heart sank, wondering if the plan she had so carefully worked out would founder stillborn. Sighing in sheer frustration, she plunged ahead.

"I talked to Glum, as he seems to know pretty much all you need to know about horses, and he said if I got used to being around horses again, then I probably wouldn't be afraid anymore."

It seemed that the tension building inside the boy was becoming unbearable. He was shifting from foot to foot as Cara talked, and now he waved his hands as though to push away her flow of words.

"What's the secret?" Richard snapped rudely.

"This." Cara nervously opened the door of the stall so that Richard could see inside.

Standing amid the straw was a wobbly foal, who backed up into the corner, staring at them with enormous brown eyes. His coat was still the downy fuzz of a newborn, although he had been weaned. He was reddish-brown, with four white stockings and a white blaze just above his right eye. Richard, who had been stiff with fear when Cara opened the box, sagged against the door at the sight of the trembling animal.

"He doesn't look so very fierce," Cara crooned, holding out a tentative hand to touch the velvety nose. "Come on, you little beauty. I won't hurt you."

Cara entered the box cautiously, clucking and crooning to the shaking colt. His coat was satiny under her caressing hands and she could feel the jump of nervous muscles. Totally ignoring Richard, Cara murmured softly to the colt and was delighted to feel him slowly steady under her fingers.

"What's his name, Miss Farraday?" Richard stood in the doorway, a longing to touch the animal etched plainly on his face.

"Glum says he hasn't got one. He said if I could think of a good one, that's what they would call him."

"It ought to be a real smasher," Richard whispered. "I think he's going to be a very special horse."

"I do, too," Cara agreed. "Now you see my secret. If you could come over with me to the stables in the morning, no one would think that I was neglecting my duties."

"I see," said Richard, eyes lighting with appreciation of the plan. Then as though he were still reluctant, he added, "I guess I could do that."

Cara spent a delightful hour grooming the colt as Richard lounged in the doorway. His eyes never left Cara, following every move she made. She never asked if he would like to help or to touch the animal, but she noted the longing in his eyes.

"Well, I think that should do it for today. Do you know, Richard, my hands aren't shaking anymore." She held them out for his inspection, then exclaimed at the amount of dirt on her hands and arms. "Could you close up the box while I locate some water?"

Cara walked down the line of stables to the trough. Unbuttoning the collar of her dress, she fanned her sweaty face with her handkerchief. Dipping it in the cold water she ran it gratefully around her neck and then, redampening it, washed her face. She made her ablutions slowly, pretending not to notice that it took Richard a long time to join her. As they left the stables, Cara waved gaily to Glum who was on the far side of the yard.

"It seems, Miss Farraday, I am forever finding you in the most unlikely of places."

Cara's head spun around at Lord Wilton's amused drawl. Under his piercing scrutiny, Cara was painfully aware of her appearance. An hour of physical labor in the close confines of the stable had done little to enhance her morning toilette. Perspiration seeped out from under her headdress and ran down her neck. Her dress was damply spotted where she had splashed water when she washed her face. In her frustration, Cara bade Julian a barely civil good morning.

"And, Richard. What brings you over here? Not planning to ride to the hounds, I presume." Julian chuckled at his own humor.

The boy's face whitened, and he clenched his fists at his sides. Without speaking he turned and left them, walking as steadily as his tear-filled eyes would permit.

"You, sir, are an insensitive boor," Cara hissed; then, as Richard disappeared from sight, she rounded on the thunderstruck Wilton, and he met the full blast of her anger. "How could you have said that? You are unspeakably the most arrogant, callous, and cruel man it has ever been my displeasure to meet." With that Cara stormed off in the direction of the Hall.

Julian stood rooted in the dust of the stable yard. No man alive had ever had the temerity to speak to him in that tone of voice, let alone an outrageous little drab of a girl whom he could crush with one hand. His scar-split eyebrow stood out against the whiteness of his face, and he plunged after Cara. As she reached the edge of the path, his hand snaked out, grasping her arm and whirling her around to face him.

"You are hurting my arm, sir."

"May I remind you, Miss Farraday, that you are a governess here only with my blessing." Julian's voice was sharp-edged steel that went totally unheeded by the angry girl.

"I don't care if you do dismiss me," Cara spat out, jerking her arm out of his grip. "I'll have my say first."

The ferocity of Cara's verbal attack totally dumbfounded Julian. He towered over the tiny girl who furiously glared up at him, hands on her hips and bosom rising and falling in her agitation. The color was high on her cheeks and her breathing came in gasps, as if she had been running. In her defense of Richard she was oblivious of her own danger. Irrelevantly Julian noticed that Cara's anger gave her skin an almost opalescent sheen.

"How dare you criticize me? When I arrived here, Belin was dressed and groomed worse than a beggar in the streets of London. And Richard was sullen and hurting because he believes that you hate him. A fine guardian you are, Your Lordship." She made of his title a scathing indictment. "Well, you may be the lord of this Hall or king of England for all I care, but in my mind you are nothing but a bully." Cara's blue-green eyes filled with unwanted tears as she glared belligerently up at Julian. Her chin quivered with emotion, but she flung her head back defiantly. "And

I don't care if you do dismiss me. I shan't take a word back." Then, before the stunned Julian could utter a word, Cara flung herself down the path to the Hall.

The veins in his temples stood out in angry relief as he glared after the girl. He smacked his riding crop into the palm of his hand, relishing the biting sting. He wished the girl were still within reach of his hands. How dare she speak to me so? he raged. He'd show her just exactly what power he possessed in his own household. He clenched his jaws, seeing again Cara's blue-green eyes blazing in contempt and her full lips set in a sneer.

"By God, I'll see her thrown out bag and baggage before this day is out," he growled.

Julian stormed back to the Hall, barging past the servants, who quickly scuttled out of the path of the angry man. He tore off his riding clothes and flung himself into the bath that his valet, Craten, had prepared for him. Despite the early hour, he bellowed for a brandy and sat in the water sipping the heady spirits.

He should have known that no good would come of his marriage to an unknown American. And now look at the fix his as yet unseen wife and the interfering duchess had gotten him into. They had foisted off on him an irresponsible, impertinent nobody who had the overpowering audacity to reproach him while she ate the very food he provided. He had definitely been in his dotage when he permitted that miniature viper to set foot in his household. He dashed off the remainder of the brandy and thrust the snifter at Craten, who hovered nervously beside the tub.

A bully! Julian swore as he took an irreverent swallow of the fresh drink. She dared to stand there in front of him with her blue-green eyes blazing fire and call *him* a bully. What nerve! "The saucy chit isn't much bigger than Belin," he growled. In fact, she had looked exactly like a child having a temper tantrum. At any minute she might have thrown herself at his feet, kicking and screaming. He chuckled at the picture that would have made. Suddenly, overcome by the humor of the entire situation, he threw his shaggy head back in a great whoop of laughter.

Tears formed in the corners of his brown eyes, and Julian sank against the back of the tub, restored to a more reasonable attitude.

The little nonentity of a governess certainly was a refreshing change from the legion of jaded or coy beauties that he had been used to dealing with. No simpering miss, our Miss Farraday. Julian grinned. It was hard for him to imagine that he had once thought she was too young and inexperienced to take over the care of his wards. He should have noted the flashing blue-green eyes during her original interview, and he might have offered her a far more interesting position in his household. He stirred uncomfortably in the water as his mind conjured up the petite body he had held in his arms and the lush mouth he had crushed against his own ravaging lips.

Remembering he was a married man, Julian tried to bring his thoughts back to a less lusty appraisal of the wench and consider the charges that she had leveled at him.

In all justice, Julian had to admit that he had been a neglectful guardian. He had been traveling abroad when word had come to him of his brother's death. He had discovered the two children were already in residence at Weathersfield when he arrived home. Unaccustomed to the company of a three-year-old and a six-year-old, he had obtained a governess and then fled to the fleshpots of London, content that he had done his duty. On his infrequent trips to the country, he had realized the children were doing poorly but had no solutions to the problem.

Belin had been confined to the nursery for the first few years, but when she emerged, she was a filthy hellion to be avoided. When he came upon her unexpectedly on the estate, she evinced some winning ways but still looked and acted like a little savage.

78

And Richard. At nine the child was a source of bafflement to Julian. He was morose and sullen. The only time that Julian had attempted to take an interest in the boy, the young cub had balked. He had tried to interest the boy in a horse of his own, but the child had cringed away in terror, earning nothing but contempt from his guardian.

Julian sipped the brandy, savoring the sharp bite of the spirits on his tongue. Miss Farraday had had some justice in her words. It was obvious that her arrival had shaken the household that Julian had ignored for so long. He wondered if all Americans were like the little governess, or if he had just had the unfortunate luck to find an extremely troublesome specimen.

His bride was an American.

If Miss Farraday was any indication of the national character, his future life would be far from tranquil. Julian enjoyed the carefree life of a bachelor and was in no hurry to give up his pleasure for the restrictions of wedded bliss. Yet, according to the duchess's letter, his bride had arrived in England. In less than a month he would be saddled with her and with an end to his freewheeling life.

When his father had broached the proposal to him, he had been surprised at the ease of his own acceptance. He had never given a great deal of thought to marriage. He knew he was expected to marry a girl of impeccable virtues and good bloodlines to carry on the name of his family. The identity of the girl had never really mattered. His brushes with the yearly line of simpering debutantes had left him with little enthusiasm for a courtship. Perhaps the very lack of a need to do the pretty had convinced him that marrying his father's choice would involve the least amount of discomfort. Others in his set had married suitably and managed to rub along well. Shrugging, Julian decided that no matter what, he would just continue his life as it had always been. Marriage need not alter anything, he reasoned wisely.

For Cara the remainder of the day dragged along sluggishly while she waited for the expected summons from Lord Wilton. She tried to enter into Belin's jubilant mood as the child paraded her carefully groomed dolls for Cara's appraisal. She must have managed well enough, for the little girl spent the remainder of the day close to her, delighting in every chore that Cara set her. After lessons and dinner and another story time in the schoolroom, it was a relief to send the children off to their beds. Then, feeling as though she could no longer breathe in the close air of her room, she threw on her cloak and ran down the stairs to the garden.

After the heat of the day, the cool evening air caressed Cara's face and soothed away the headache that furrowed her brow. She pressed her fingers along the edges of her headdress, wishing that she might free her hair to blow in the soft breeze. She reveled in the moist, perfumed air as she walked along the dark paths in the garden. The flowered borders were merely shadowed clumps, with an occasional spot of brilliant color caught in a wandering moonbeam. There was enough light for her to walk the gravel paths without worrying about stumbling.

Why had Julian not dismissed her? Cara wondered in puzzlement.

By all rights he should have, she admitted. She was thoroughly annoyed with herself for having lost her temper. However, she had been furious when he had spoken so insensitively to Richard, and no power on earth could have stilled her tongue. She knew her grandmother would be justifiably shocked at her behavior. Cara was so deep in thought that she failed to hear the light step behind her until a hand fell on her shoulder and she gasped in terror.

"Your pardon, Miss Farraday, I did not mean to startle you."

In the moonlight Cara recognized Edward Tallworth's

slender figure. She crossed her arms over her breast trying to calm her rapid breathing and laughed shakily to dispel her uneasiness at the man's sudden appearance.

"It's just that I thought I was alone in the garden, Sir Edward."

Cara felt nervous in Tallworth's presence. There was a certain lazy immorality to the manner in which his eyes roamed over her body that she found disturbing. Cara pulled away from his hand and gathered her cloak more securely around her.

"Such a lovely night for a walk outdoors," Tallworth announced.

"Yes. I have found the evening very refreshing."

"Perhaps you wouldn't mind if I walked with you for a while?" Tallworth questioned.

"I—I was just on my way back to the Hall," Cara blurted in a rush of words.

For some reason she did not exactly trust Tallworth's company, unchaperoned in a dark garden. Perhaps it was the vague whispers she had heard about the fate of the last governess, but for whatever reasons, Cara had no intention of putting herself into another compromising position.

"A short walk would be quite pleasant," Tallworth continued, as though he had not heard her reply. Taking her arm, he turned her in the direction away from the Hall.

Cara stiffened in the man's grasp. She was unwilling to create a scene by struggling with her companion, and so let him hold her elbow. Tallworth's rapier-thin body moved easily, displaying an athlete's agility and wiriness. Despite her uneasiness, Cara assumed he was a gentleman and that she could count on his behaving as such. Mentally shrugging away her apprehension, she gracefully followed his lead.

"Are you enjoying your lessons with the children?" he questioned.

Although Cara sensed that Sir Edward was less that interested in her schoolroom activities, she chattered brightly about the children. She knew that she was babbling but felt compelled to keep up a light social conversation. A feeling of dread washed over Cara's body as she realized Tallworth's steps were leading toward the maze in the center of the garden. She berated herself for permitting the situation to get away from her control. She should have followed her first instincts and broken away from the man at their first encounter. Her heart beat raggedly as she determined to sever the contact before she found herself in worse difficulties.

"I'm sorry, Sir Edward, but I should like to return to the Hall." Cara attempted to keep her voice cool and impersonal.

"Really, Miss Farraday, you needn't come the coy miss with me." Tallworth's voice was hoarse in the quiet garden. "You have yet to see the maze by moonlight."

"I have no intention of going to the maze with you."

"Then perhaps we should sit here instead."

Before Cara could react, Tallworth pulled her down onto a stone seat beside the path. His arms were immediately around her, imprisoning her with bands of steel against his chest. She struggled uselessly against the confinement until she heard the loathsome man chuckle at her helplessness.

"If you don't let me go this minute, I will scream loud enough to wake the entire household," Cara said, gritting out the words through clenched teeth. Although it was true she was frightened, uppermost in her emotions was a furious core of anger that the man would dare to treat her in such a cavalier fashion.

"Do you really want everyone to know that you have been in the garden with me?" Tallworth asked, his eyebrow raised in mockery.

Cara bit her lip in her frustration. She would die before letting Julian find her in another awkward situation. Damning men in general and Tallworth in particular, she began to struggle anew.

In an instant Cara realized that her strength was inadequate against Sir Edward's athletic build. Frantically she searched for a way out of this frightening assault. Tallworth pressed her body backward until she was almost lying on the bench. Taking a chance, Cara let her body go limp. Accepting this as a sign of her surrender, Sir Edward loosened his grip and prepared to conduct his seduction more slowly. As his hands reached for the hem of her skirt, Cara rolled sideways, knocking the man off the bench as she sprang to her feet, preparing to run.

A rasping cough cut through Tallworth's cursing as he staggered after the girl. The two protagonists halted, frozen by the unknown presence in the garden.

"Begging your pardon, Sir Edward, but Miss Farraday's wanted at the Hall."

"Who's there?" Tallworth snarled.

"Pennyfeather, sir" came the reply.

The giant stepped closer so that the moonlight glinted off his grizzled hair and seamed face. He ignored Cara totally, although he was aware of her every breath. The air in the garden pulsed with the tension between the three figures, each of them a statue in a tableau.

"It's Belin, Miss Farraday," Pennyfeather mumbled, breaking the spell. "She's woke up with a powerful nightmare and is carrying on somethin' awful. Mrs. Clayton thought as how you would be able to settle her down."

"Of course, Pennyfeather. I'll come back with you at once." Cara drew her cloak around her as she passed the malevolent figure on the bench. "Good night, Sir Edward."

As she hurried along the paths toward the Hall, Cara felt hot tears roll down her cheeks. She wanted nothing more than to throw herself into Pennyfeather's arms and sob out her fear and anger. Almost as though the enormous man recognized her need, he placed a fatherly paw on her shoulder and slowed his pace.

"Just take some deep breaths, and it'll be better," Pennyfeather suggested, as though to a frightened child.

Cara followed his advice and was surprised that she did, in fact, feel better. She turned to the older man and smiled shakily. "Thank you, Pennyfeather. I was incredibly stupid," Cara chastised herself. "I thought Tallworth was more of a gentleman. Apparently I was mistaken."

"Just remember that there's no animal in the woods that you can ever fully trust." Then the man gave a throaty chuckle as he looked down at the young woman. " 'Sides, miss, you didn't appear to need much help. Once you broke his grip, it was clear sailing. You could always outrun him."

At the hint of amusement in the old poacher's voice, Cara managed a watery giggle. Her mood immediately lightened, and they walked to the Hall in companionable silence. At the door to the children's wing, Cara held out her hand in thanks. "Should I check on Belin before I go to bed?"

"No, miss. The child sleeps ever so soundly now that you've come to the Hall." Touching two fingers to his cap, Pennyfeather slid silently back toward the woods.

Chapter Six

The sun, only minutes old, was visible as a promise above the line of trees as Cara hurried out to the stables. Glum stood patiently in the stable yard, holding the reins of a slim-legged mare. Since the beginning of her experiment with Richard and the colt, the wizened head groom had been eager to set Cara on only the best of Julian's cattle. Preferring to ride at dawn before the rest of the household was about, she managed to secure a carefree hour to herself before she had to take on the restrictions imperative in her role as a proper governess. Somehow, after the morning ride Cara was able to fulfill her duties without chafing under the confinement of her designated role.

"It's going to be a beautiful summer's day, Glum," Cara stated, gently rubbing the mare's nose, "Morning, Gentian."

"She's a mite frisky this morning," Glum cautioned. "Better let her run a bit before you put her to any of those jumps."

Although his gruff voice held disapproval, the twinkle in his eyes belied the words. Cara had infinite respect for the venerable horseman and realized the compliment he paid her by letting her ride the horses unattended. Although she had ridden others, she had come to love the dainty little

Gentian, whose mischievous streak turned every ride into a challenge.

"Now, Glum, you know I'll treat her like the lady she is," Cara said straight-facedly. "Actually, Gentian and I have worked out a very nice arrangement. She gets to have her way on the ride out, and I get to have my way coming back to the stables."

At Glum's snort of mirth, Cara gave him a dazzling smile, warm and free of restraint. The old man cocked his head to the side, studying the girl covertly as she patted and caressed the mare. It always surprised him that no one had been able to discern the beauty of the girl despite the dowdy clothes and the all-encompassing headdress. It amused him when she arrived at the stable, all bland looks and prim airs, in case anyone was near. When they were alone, the girl opened up, making him privy to the warm-hearted natural grace beneath the fusty disguise. He supposed that it was necessary to hide her looks in order to hire out as governess, but it certainly was a shame.

Glum nested his fingers to give the girl a leg up, marveling at the featherweight in his hands. He watched critically while Cara arranged her knee on the sidesaddle and smoothed the skirts of her oversize riding habit. Despite its poor fit, the dove-gray color became her, Glum noted. As the girl and the mare trotted sedately out of the yard, the groom shook his head, knowing that just beyond the band of trees that hid them from sight, they would be flying along the track that led to the high fields. His leathery skin wrinkled in amusement as he remembered the first time Cara had ridden out.

Glum had followed the girl that first morning. Unsure of Caroline's expertise and concerned for Wilton's bloodstock, he had remained discreetly out of sight and had almost stumbled on her when she stopped at the trees lining the first clearing. Easing himself into the sheltering underbrush, Glum had moved silently to the edge of the opening.

His old eyes had almost started out of his head when the governess pulled off her headdress to display a wealth of burnished curls that fluttered like a pennant as she raced across the field.

Thoroughly intrigued, Glum had followed Cara to the high fields, staying well within the cover of trees as he watched her. In growing respect he had observed the care with which she worked the horse. Each tested the other for weakness, but the young woman always maintained a firm control. Finally both the governess and the horse rode as a single unit. Her jumping skills were apparent as she started slowly and then increased the height of the jumps until she felt the horse hesitate. Then, leaping off the horse's back, she rubbed the sweating animal with sweet-smelling clumps of grass, humming softly as she worked. From that day on, Glum never worried when the girl rode out in the morning.

Unaware of Glum's reminiscing, Cara and Gentian sniffed gratefully at the dewy smell filling their nostrils. As the track wound up through the woods, the gray capered freely under Cara's relaxed rein. When they reached the high field, the mare, accustomed to the routine, stood whickering gently as Cara untied her loathsome headdress and unbound her hair. In the quiet of the early morning, she was free of the restriction of her self-imposed disguise. For an hour she was back again in America, riding her father's horses, hair flying loosely in the summer wind.

"Hold on a minute, Gentian." Cara laughed as the dainty mare stamped impatiently. "We'll be off soon enough."

Cara ran her fingers through her hair, letting the riot of red-gold curls tumble unchecked down her back. Her head felt lighter, free of the weighty braid of hair she had to bind close against the nape of her neck. It was the part of playing the frumpy governess she hated the most. Unbuttoning the collar of her habit she stretched her neck trying to catch the morning breeze on her perspiring throat.

"What a perfectly wonderful morning." Cara sighed.

At the unladylike snort of annoyance from her companion, Cara kneed the mare into a gentle trot as she breathed in the fresh air, her mind busy with her own thoughts.

It had been over a week since she had had her angry confrontation with Julian in the stable yard. It still amazed her that he hadn't dismissed her out of hand for her ill-advised verbal attack. Since then, Cara had tried to maintain exemplary decorum, but she was aware of his disapproving eyes following her whenever they chanced to meet. She was thankful he had not summoned the children for a further audience.

Gentian blew impatiently, the muscles under her skin jumping to indicate her readiness for a more vigorous workout. With a start, Cara brought her mind back to the business at hand. She settled herself more securely in the sidesaddle, then nudged the mare into a blur of movement. Tearing across the fields and up into the flatter meadows, Cara reveled in the wind against her face. The blood pulsed in her veins as she blended with the movement of the horse, giving Gentian her head, although directing the horse to the area where the jumps were located.

Julian usually did not ride at such an unconscionably early hour. However, since his houseguests had all abandoned him, leaving him to rusticate in the country, he had been rising early. He did not miss them; he had to admit that their continued company had begun to pall on him. Since he had been at Weathersfield, he was becoming more interested in the property. Perhaps he ought to spend more time on the estate, despite the lures cast out by the departing Valencia.

"Darling, you can't possibly stay here," the blond girl had drawled coquettishly, peeping at him beguilingly through a flutter of eyelashes. "The Regent and simply

88

everyone will be in Brighton. Couldn't you possibly come with us?''

''Really, Valencia. You needn't carry on so. I'm sure you will have gallants aplenty to hover around you,'' he had countered.

''But, Julian, I'll miss you.''

Julian had been surprised to discover that he was quite impervious to the pleading tones of the golden girl framed in the carriage window. She had always preened and pouted to force him to do her bidding. He knew that there were others who had sampled the delights of the winsome girl posed as a picture of wounded innocence. Her kittenish ways had amused him in the past, but now he wished an end to her guises and false emotions. He shrugged off a vision of angry blue-green eyes as he softly kissed the wrist of Valencia's regally extended hand.

''Truly, my dear, I must be about my estate. I have been lamentably neglectful of my household and my tenants,'' Julian had argued reasonably.

It was true, Julian thought, as he sat his horse on the edge of the clearing. Since his houseguests had left, he had delved more heavily than usual into the business of the estate. He had always been conscientious about his holdings but had left a great portion of the details to his agents. Lately he had become aware that he ought to spend more time on his estate. Perhaps he had become bored with the social set in London. He had felt a building ennui which had surprisingly dissipated as he became more immersed in the day-to-day events on his property.

If only Edward Tallworth had left with the others, Julian's peace of mind would be complete. He was aware that the man was bored by his sudden enjoyment of estate business, but Tallworth still lounged around, unwilling to accept the hints thrown out to take himself off. Though Tallworth grumbled and complained about the country hours and lack of entertainment, he had made no move to find more kindred spirits.

Julian's quiet reverie was shattered as a horse bolted through a thin band of trees to his right.

The sudden appearance of the horse and rider had an almost magical quality. Under cover of the trees, Julian watched as the rider set the gray to the first set of jumps. At first, he believed that the rider was a child, but on closer scrutiny he realized it was a young girl. Her figure, almost at one with the horse, appeared to be slender, but the swell of bosom indicated more mature characteristics. Sun-burnished curls blew behind her like a shaft of fire. Although at this distance Julian could not make out her features, he sensed that she was a rare beauty.

As each of the obstacles was successfully jumped, a tinkling sound of pure joy floated across the field.

With bated breath Julian watched in fascination as the twosome sailed majestically over the low hedges, working deliberately toward the stone wall set at the far end of the meadow. The girl approached the high jump but did not try it immediately. She walked the mare along the wall, talking and patting the neck of the sweating animal. Then Julian heard a low chuckle as the girl swerved away from the stones and trotted on the capering little gray down the field. Horse and rider thundered toward the wall, and Julian held his breath as the mare's muscles bunched for the jump. At the last minute the mare shied, swerving abruptly and dumping her rider in a flurry of skirts.

Expelling his breath in a quick explosion, Julian dug his heels into the sides of his stallion.

Cara tested her limbs and was grateful to discover nothing but her pride was injured. She ruefully rubbed her grass-stained hands against her skirts, then approached the leisurely grazing gray.

"You ungrateful hussy," Cara grumbled, reaching for

the reins. "After all the apples and sweets I've given you. That's the third time this week you've refused the wall. One of these days you'll have to take it, you know."

The mare nuzzled Cara's shoulder by way of apology, and the disheveled girl affectionately stroked the neck of the beautiful animal. As she leaned over to brush the dirt off her riding habit, she heard the sound of an approaching horse. In alarm she squinted at the figure at the far end of the field, recognizing Julian even at that distance. Without thought Cara grasped Gentian's reins and standing on a nearby stump catapulted herself into the saddle. Fear of discovery set Cara's heart pounding, but she forced down her emotion as she once more rode the mare at the wall.

"Trust me, sweetheart," Cara crooned into Gentian's ear as they pounded across the field toward the rough pile of stones. "We can make it."

The horse must have sensed Cara's desperation, because her muscles bunched and without hesitation she took the wall with inches to spare. In full flight the horse and rider raced for the trees and disappeared.

At first Julian was genuinely stunned by the flight of the girl, but his amazement quickly turned to anger. By the time he cleared the wall, there was no evidence of the pair. Rider and horse had been swallowed up in the woods, with no indication of their direction. From the high fields, Julian knew, the girl had access to limitless areas. He was furious that an unknown rider was on his property, but having no idea which estate she had come from, there was no way to intercept her. In exasperation he pushed his hair off his sweating forehead, slapping his riding crop viciously against his boot.

In near panic Cara rode through the woods, stopping only when she feared that she would do Gentian some damage. She sat atop the heaving horse, listening for any signs of pursuit. With shaking hands she braided her hair and retied the headdress to cover it. Brushing the worst of the dirt from her skirts, Cara tried to compose herself before she approached the stable yard. She knew she was still in imminent danger of discovery should Julian run into her at this juncture. Despite the minutes ticking away, she waited until Gentian had rested before nudging the mare along the path to the stables.

"Not hurt, miss?" Glum asked in concern, taking in Cara's dirt-streaked habit.

"No, it's worse," cried the flustered girl, leaping lightly to the ground. "It's Lord Wilton. He—I mean," the governess stammered in confusion.

"I'll take care of Gentian. Off with ye."

Glum caught the reins thrust hastily into his callused hands, then turned with the mare as Cara fled toward the Hall. Moving quickly to get the horse under cover, Glum assigned a boy to walk and groom the horse. He was back outside when the darkly scowling Lord Wilton returned.

Julian flung himself from the horse, turning toward the Hall. He hesitated, then stopped and hailed Glum, who was leading the stallion toward the stables. "Have you seen any strangers hereabouts?"

"No one's arrived at the Hall since you went off for your ride, Lord Wilton."

"Actually it's a girl I'm wondering about," Julian mentioned nonchalantly.

"One of the tenants' girls, milord?" Glum squinted into the sun, then spat in the dust.

"No. It's a young gentlewoman with blazing red hair, who rides like the wind. I could swear I've never seen her around here before. She was up riding in the high meadow, and then she vanished."

"What kind of a horse be she riding?" Glum asked with apparent interest.

"I don't know. It was gray, but I really didn't get a very close look at it."

"Well, I can ask some of the boys." Glum's lackluster tone indicated the probable failure of such a plan.

"Do that," Julian commanded. Then, in a more offhand tone of voice, he continued, "It's not really important. I just thought it was passing strange finding an unknown girl on my land."

So that's the way of it, Glum thought, staring apprehensively at Julian's disappearing back. No wonder Miss Farraday was in such a lather. Almost caught. The worst of it was that Wilton had failed to recognize the mare. With his love and appreciation of horses, he was usually able to spot and identify most animals at a great distance. Glum had to admit that Miss Farraday made a breathtaking picture when she was astride a horse. He could understand why Wilton had had eyes for nothing but the girl.

Shaking his head worriedly, Glum stomped toward the stables. "There's always trouble when the stallions are in rut," the head groom prophesied gloomily.

Julian, unaware of Glum's dire predictions, sat long over his breakfast coffee contemplating the girl in the woods.

Even at a distance, Julian had recognized that the girl was gentry. She was mounted on prime stock. The gray had taken the fences on delicate legs, and its lines were good. Julian had taken that much in unconsciously. No tenant's daughter had a horse of that caliber. But it was her ability to ride, jumping sidesaddle, by God, that labeled her as a member of his own class. He wondered what had made the girl bolt so suddenly. Perhaps she was staying at one of the estates, wandered too far afield, and then had been frightened when Julian approached.

Sipping unconsciously the cold coffee, Julian thought it might be a good idea to become reacquainted with some of his neighbors.

After all, now that he was planning to spend more time on the estate, Julian felt that it would be politic to visit some of the other landowners to exchange ideas. It would

93

be splendid if he could locate other children the same age as Belin and Richard, he rationalized. Perhaps during the visits he would be able to smoke out the girl in the woods. Mentally he ran through the names of his neighbors, trying to remember if any of them had older daughters or young wives. There was something about the red-haired horse-woman that struck him as familiar. He hadn't been close enough to observe her features clearly, but he had the distinct feeling that he had seen her somewhere before. She definitely owed him an apology for dashing off as she had, Julian thought, eyes narrowed to angry slits. He would find that girl if he had to visit every estate in the county.

He slammed his fist onto the table, setting the china to trembling. Why now, when he should be contemplating the coming joys of marital bliss, did this girl have to turn up? Even the brief glimpse that he had of the beautiful wood sprite promised a fascination he was loath to ignore. At any rate, it would do no harm to find the girl, if only to appease his curiosity.

"Can we, Miss Farraday?" Belin asked. "Just for to-day?"

"I'm sorry, Belin. I'm afraid I wasn't attending." Cara sat up straighter and tried to bring her mind back to the breakfast table conversation.

"I just wanted to know if we could read today instead of doing sums." Belin's voice was exasperated as she repeated the question. "It's started to rain, and it's too gloomy to do sums."

"Admit it, Belin. Even if it were sunny, you'd rather do anything than sums," was Richard's brotherly observation.

Cara looked outside, surprised that the day had turned so rainy. It made a perfect compliment to her mood, which fluctuated between fear of discovery and general gloom.

"Can we, Miss Farraday?"

"I'm sorry, Belin," Cara apologized again to the child. "I think reading would be a grand idea. In fact, if you wanted to pick out a book, I'm sure that Richard would read it to you."

"She always picks out baby books," Richard complained.

"I do not!"

"You do so!"

Cara settled the argument by picking out a book of Viking adventures with enough battles to keep Richard contented and yet with simple enough stories to entertain Belin. Once the children became engrossed in the book, Cara slumped in dejection on the window seat. She stared blindly out the rain-spattered glass, her mind whirling over the events of her morning ride.

Since she hadn't been summoned by Julian, it was apparent that he had not recognized her in the woods.

Her body trembled at the near discovery. She could just imagine his glowering looks as he demanded an explanation. With unrelenting determination, Julian would have the story of her deception before he was done interrogating her. Her mind conjured up a vision of the angry interview, and she winced at the all-too-real possibility.

Worst of all, Julian would once again have found her in another untenable position, disheveled, sweaty, and reeking of horse. Cara didn't know why that should bother her so. But she did know, she admitted miserably, staring with unseeing eyes at the rain-drenched world beyond the schoolroom. She was in love with Julian.

"It's just not possible," Cara muttered under her breath.

She couldn't be in love with Julian; she didn't even like him. He was arrogant, autocratic, stubborn, and a bully. She was offended by his easy morals and furious at his neglect of the children. Yet every time she encountered him, she found herself drawn to the magnetism of his personality. "I must have some character weakness," Cara fumed bitterly. After all, there was absolutely nothing laudable about her husband.

Unfortunately her eyes remembered how Julian's tousled black hair fell across his forehead, just waiting for a soft hand to brush it back. Her lips remembered the soft firmness of Julian's mouth pressed against her own, calling forth an unknown response. Her body remembered the rippling strength of his body as his lean length supported her quivering weight. Cara stifled a groan, trying to banish her memories.

In her heart she knew that it was dangerous to remain at Weathersfield. Not only did she have the fear of discovery to contend with but her situation was no longer safe with Edward Tallworth still in residence. After Tallworth's aborted assault in the garden she had taken particular care to avoid him. Whenever she had crossed his path, she felt his eyes burning into her. His hawklike observation warned his prey that he was only biding his time.

Yet despite all the dangers, she couldn't leave. The children needed her. Cara had to admit that she had come to love them dearly. Belin was thriving under her care, but she needed more time with Richard. She had finally won his confidence, and she couldn't afford to have any changes shake the foundation of that trust. Her sudden disappearance would inevitably undo all the progress Richard had made. And he really had made progress.

Both Cara and Glum had hoped that Richard would lose his fear of horses by being around the gentle little colt. But neither of them had expected the experiment to work so quickly. After two days Richard was running to fetch the brushes and extra feed that had been mysteriously left in other parts of the stable. Hurrying back and forth amid the normal activity of the yard, the boy seemed unaffected by the presence of the other horses. On the third day Cara stumbled on her way to the box.

"Are you all right, Miss Farraday?" Richard's voice

was filled with concern as he bent over the recumbent form of his governess.

"Fine, Richard. At least, I think so."

Cara stood up, shaking out her dusty skirts and brushing at the dirt on her hands. The boy stood quietly while she examined her booted foot, testing it gingerly on the oak flooring.

"There. I'm sure my ankle is perfectly sound," Cara announced, staggering a little as she hobbled toward the last stall. "Perhaps if I sat down a moment. I still feel a little shaky."

The boy fluttered solicitously around her as she sat on a bale of hay, her foot propped up on a grain barrel. He was unaware of the calculating look his governess cast him under her fringe of lashes.

"Can I get you anything, Miss Farraday?"

"I don't think so, Richard. I just need a moment to catch my breath."

"You took quite a tumble. I think you ought to just sit there and rest. I could groom the colt today," Richard offered.

"Really, I'm sure I will be fine. Besides, I would be shirking my duties." Cara forced a note of wistfulness into her voice. "It's very hard work for a young lad."

"I'd try ever so hard. I've been watching you every day." Richard was desperate to convince his governess. "You could watch everything and tell me if I forgot anything."

"Yes, I can see that might work," Cara agreed finally.

In recompense for Richard's labor, Cara suggested that he might like to name the colt. It had taken several days of frowning concentration before the boy was contented with a name.

"Do you think Loki would be a suitable name?" Richard asked. He rushed on before Cara could offer an opinion. "I got the idea when you were reading that Norse

97

book. It's the name of the god of mischief. I thought it might be a good name yesterday when he butted you in the stomach.''

"I see nothing funny about that incident, you loathsome child. A true gentleman would refrain from mentioning it.'' Cara failed to control the twitching of her lips and joined Richard as he burst into laughter.

So Loki had been named, and from then on Richard took over the grooming chores while Cara lounged in the doorway or wandered through the stables talking to the other horses. After discussing possible choices, she and Glum had picked out a sweet-tempered hunter for Richard's first ride. With any luck, the boy could be coaxed to accompany Cara at the end of the week.

But with a sinking heart Cara acknowledged that if she gained the time to help Richard, she might yet lose everything.

Chapter Seven

Laying the book down on the bench, Cara stretched her arms over her head, easing the strain of muscles across her shoulders. She yawned, letting her eyes roam lazily over the garden. Having eaten more than usual at lunch, she was paying the price with a sluggishness that seeped into her bones. Her eyes following the path of a bee dipping from flower to flower, but even that activity failed to rouse her out of the sun-induced lethargy into which she had fallen. Sighing, she leaned against the cool marble back of the bench.

After only two weeks at Weathersfield, she felt as though she had spent a lifetime in its sheltered atmosphere. It was true that many of her days were fraught with indecision and the possible danger of exposure. On the whole, however, she had never felt as contented as she did now. For months in America, and then on the voyage across the Atlantic, she had been distraught by the death of her father and by the incredibility of her marriage to Julian. But looking back to her first days at the Hall, she could see that she had felt welcome from the beginning. Her days had been full of the children, and then more and more her thoughts had been taken up with Julian.

Cara's eyes flew open as a shiver coursed through her body.

Just thinking about the man could totally disorient her. Cara had admitted that she loved him but the passion engendered by his presence in her thoughts or in person was a source of confusion. Generally ruled by her common sense, the loss of control when confronted by Julian was a new and uncomfortable sensation. She remembered how scornfully she had viewed her friends who were in the early stages of a love affair. Since she had met Julian, her emotions had been turned upside down, leaving her feeling graceless and schoolgirlish. Cara wished for the simpler emotion of anger that Julian had filled her with instead of the breathless, heart-stopping whirl she had been in lately.

Glancing at the watch pinned to her bodice, she cocked her head, listening for the sounds of the children. She picked up the poetry book and stuffed it into the capacious pockets of her blue gabardine dress. Smoothing her scarf, she checked for stray strands of hair and, finding some, tucked them under its edge. Then, leisurely strolling through the garden, she headed for the wilder woods around the lake.

"Belin! Richard!" Cara smiled, wondering if the children were hiding, lying in wait to leap out and scare her.

Leaving the manicured paths in the garden, she entered the woods. She stood quietly, letting her eyes get used to the dimmer light after the glaring sunshine of the garden. Then, walking briskly along the path, she called for the children. Perspiration broke out on her forehead as the path wound steadily uphill. Rounding a slight crest she saw Belin's tiny figure running toward her. Cara's heart gave a frightened lurch at the tears on the child's face, and she hurried to meet the little girl.

"What is it, Belin?" Cara asked anxiously as the child stumbled against her.

"Come. Oh, Miss Farraday, please come."

Cara knelt down in the dirt holding the girl's trembling body tightly, waiting for the rasping breath to ease. It was obvious that something had badly frightened Belin, and Cara worried that Richard might be in trouble. Cara bit her lip impatiently biding her time until the child could control her breathing enough to speak.

"Oh, Miss Farraday. You've got to come," Belin finally gasped out. "He's caught in one of the traps."

"Richard?" Cara asked in horror.

"No. Pennyfeather. Hurry."

The child, nearly hysterical with fear, grabbed Cara's hand, dragging her along the path deeper into the woods. It was only a matter of moments before they came upon the scene of the accident.

A white-faced Richard knelt beside Pennyfeather, whose leg was caught between the teeth of one of the poaching traps. Beside the old man was a shotgun and a brace of rabbits. The shrewd brown eyes in the sun-bronzed face looked up guiltily into Cara's horrified ones.

"I told the wee ones to leave me to meself, mum," Pennyfeather rasped out hoarsely.

"Hush, Pennyfeather. I'm glad they came for me." Cara moistened her suddenly dry lips and asked, "How bad is it?"

"Thank the Lord, it's an old trap. I don't think it's broken my leg, but it's swole up mighty fine."

Cara knelt beside the old man, looking carefully at the ancient cast-iron trap. The trap was a cruelly ingenious device used by many gamekeepers to discourage poachers. To arm the device, the two half circles lined with teeth were laid flat and set in place. Covered with leaves, the trap lay dormant until stepped upon. Then the half circles sprang up, settling their teeth in the poacher's leg. The trap itself was chained to a tree, so there was no possibility of carrying the man away without first loosening the trap.

"How long before the gamekeeper gets here?"

" 'Bout another fifteen minutes. Thirty at the most."

Despite the fact that a poacher stayed on the move when

he was hunting, the shots were generally heard by the gamekeeper. Then a group was formed to check the woods. If caught, the consequences for the poacher would be dire. By Pennyfeather's reckoning, there was not much time left. Looking across the recumbent man, Cara stared into Richard's tear-filled eyes. Behind her, Cara could hear Belin's pathetic sniffling.

"Richard, I want you to take the gun to Pennyfeather's cottage. If you run into anyone, just tell them you found it." Cara searched the boy's face for signs of understanding, but his eyes were fastened on the injured man, oblivious of her voice. "Richard! You must listen to me."

Slowly Richard's glazed eyes focused on Cara's face, and she repeated her instructions slowly until she was sure that he had fully understood. Shaking his head to clear it, he staggered awkwardly to his feet.

"Take Belin with you. It won't help matters if you're found here. Get along now," she ordered as the children hesitated.

Richard picked up the gun, moving as though his whole body was weighted down. The boy stood beside Cara looking forlornly at his friend. Then, biting his lip, he reached out his hand to Belin and trudged toward the path that would lead to Pennyfeather's cottage.

Once the children were taken care of, Cara fought to free her mind so that she could think clearly. If it could be avoided, she wanted to keep Pennyfeather out of the hands of the law. Standing up, she searched around the brush until she found a stout branch. She smashed it against a tree trunk until it broke into two pieces. Although she was aware of the time rapidly ticking away, she fought to keep her movements slow and steady. Taking one of the pieces of the branch, Cara slid it between the two sets of teeth. Keeping the stick parallel with the ground, she stood up and placed her feet on either end of the branch, pinning the one side of the trap to the ground.

Cara's stomach lurched with nausea, and sweat broke out on her upper lip, but she steadied herself as the poacher's brown eyes lifted to hers. If she acted impersonally enough, she would be able to close her mind to the blood and torn flesh on Pennyfeather's leg. Ignoring the pain etched into the giant's face, she spoke briskly and matter-of-factly.

"I'm going to try to use the other branch as a lever. Will you be able to pull your foot out?"

Slowly the old man pushed himself up to a sitting position, taking most of the weight on his hands. He put the boot on his free leg against the edge of the trap. Gritting his teeth, he grinned lopsidedly at Cara and raised a tufted eyebrow as if in answer to her question.

Wedging the other branch against the upper half circle of the trap, she pushed against the ground, trying to pry apart the two sets of teeth. At first nothing happened. Her sweating hands slipped a little on the bark of the branch, and Cara quickly wrapped a corner of her dress around it to get a better purchase. Then, grabbing hold again, she took a huge gulp of air and pushed on the branch. The muscles across her back stretched painfully, and slowly the jaws began to spread apart. Inch by inch the opening widened. Every muscle in Cara's body screamed as she strained.

"Now, Pennyfeather!"

Pushing with his free foot, Pennyfeather slowly began to withdraw his leg. Watching the gradual progress, Cara prayed for strength. Suddenly her muscles gave out and the trap snapped shut. It bit on empty air, jerking backward and hitting her a nasty blow on the ankle. With a gasping sigh, Cara lost her balance and fell in a heap on the leafy ground.

"Are you hurt, miss?"

Pennyfeather's voice was hoarse with pain, but at least he was free of the trap. Cara sat still for a moment, taking a mental inventory. Aside from a bruise or two from her fall, her ankle was the only real injury. Staggering up, she knelt beside Pennyfeather.

"I suspect we'll both live. But we'd better get out of here before we have to face Lord Wilton."

Gingerly Cara pulled the material away from Pennyfeather's wound. His leg was bleeding profusely. Tearing off the edge of her petticoat, she bound the leg to temporarily staunch the flow of blood. After all her effort, she knew they couldn't afford to leave a trail of gore to Pennyfeather's cottage. Cautiously she helped the old man to his feet. Her own ankle pained her, but at least she was able to stand on it. Although he protested, Pennyfeather finally accepted Cara's shoulder to lean on as they made their painful progress down the trail.

The children saw them coming and raced out to offer their help. Fluttering around their injured friend, they generally got in the way, but Cara was too tired to discourage them.

"Belin, get some rags to clean the wound and, Richard, you get me some water."

Cara was breathless with the unusual exertion as she lowered Pennyfeather into a chair beside the banked fire. Wearily she sagged against a table, waiting for her hammering heart to slow. Tentatively she wiggled her ankle, ignoring the throbbing pain as the relief that it wasn't broken washed over her. Looking down at herself, she winced at the picture she must make. Her dress was sweat-stained and streaked with dirt, and a small patch of blood smudged the hem. Perspiration ran down her face and her hands were scratched and dirty. Her eyes stared across at the old man whose mouth twitched as though he were sharing her joke. Smiling back, she pushed herself away from the table.

"All right, you old wretch. Where do you keep the gin?"

Although the poacher was at first hesitant, under Cara's

glowering look he yielded with a grimace. Disgruntledly he indicated a corner of the room behind some pans and other odds and ends. Rummaging for the jug, Cara found it and brought it to the table, where her patient eyed it longingly. Although Pennyfeather tried to push her away, Cara knelt on the beaten-earth floor and with the aid of a knife ripped his buckskins to expose the wound.

She had to swallow convulsively several times before she was able to continue her inspection. The teeth from the trap had gouged holes in both sides of the leg, which itself was quite swollen and bruised-looking. With gentle motions she washed away the dirt and caked blood, watching anxiously as fresh blood rose cleanly to the surface. Then bracing his leg across her thigh, she uncorked the bottle of gin and poured it liberally across the wounds.

Although Pennyfeather had remained quiet throughout her ministrations, he sucked in his breath as the alcohol stung the wound. He's probably angry at the waste of good gin, Cara thought unsympathetically. Looking up at the man, she grinned at his expression of disgust.

"I didn't use it all."

Cara proffered the jug which Pennyfeather raised in his pawlike hand and swallowed greedily. He wiped his mouth on his sleeve, grinning back at the girl as he cradled the jug against his chest.

"Promise me that you'll have this leg looked at, Pennyfeather," Cara pleaded as she eased his leg to the ground.

"I'll have Megan see to it when she comes in the morning."

Cara knew that one of the tenant's wives brought over a kettle for Pennyfeather's dinner each day. She had met the woman several times when in the company of the children and had taken a liking to the shy, soft-spoken woman. She knew that Megan would have salves and ointments to heal the man's leg. Nodding her head in acquiescence, she rose to her feet as Pennyfeather took another long swig from the bottle.

"And, furthermore, I want your promise that you'll not take the children with you if you go poaching."

"Oh, Miss Farraday, it wasn't Pennyfeather's fault," Richard burst in. "Belin and I just happened to run across him right before the accident."

"It's not to happen again. I don't approve of the poaching laws, but you'll have to abide by them." Then, as the boy looked mutinous, Cara continued softly. "That could have been Belin's leg caught in the trap today."

At the startled look in the boy's eyes, Cara turned her back on him. At least that would give him food for thought, she reasoned silently. Richard would never give up the opportunity for adventure on his own account, but he would protect Belin from possible harm.

"Is Pennyfeather going to be able to walk again?" Belin asked in a whisper.

Cara's heart turned over at the woebegone face raised to hers. Tearstains ran down dirty cheeks, leaving trails of whiter skin. Taking a corner of the cloth, Cara dipped it in water and washed the little girl's face. Satisfied at last, she hugged the child and pushed her toward Richard.

"Now you two get back to the Hall. The excitement is over for the day."

After bidding Pennyfeather a hasty good-bye and promising to return the next day for a visit, the children scampered off down the track toward the Hall. Cara turned in the doorway to see Pennyfeather taking another long pull at the jug. His smile was a trifle crooked, and his eyes had a groggy look to them.

"I'll go back along the path and make sure there's nothing there to send the gamekeeper to your door."

"Much obliged, miss," Pennyfeather slurred softly as he shifted uncomfortably in his chair.

"It's nothing, you old reprobate. You've been a good friend to the children. And to me," she added.

With a final wave of her hand, Cara left the cottage, hobbling painfully on her ankle. Once out of sight of the cottage, she pulled up the hem of her dress to look at the bruise on her leg.

The ankle was puffy and discolored, but no skin had been broken. Although it was swollen, she suspected after a thorough soaking and a good night's rest, it would be fine. But for now she had a painful walk ahead of her. Despite her slow pace, it was no time at all until she found the place where the accident had happened.

The rabbits lay on the ground just off the path. Fearing their discovery, Cara gingerly picked them up and carried them into the woods. She was dismayed at the amount of blood on the ground. Dropping the rabbits, she broke off a small tree branch and began to sweep the area. Cautiously she picked up the trap, ready to shove it under a thick covering of leaves. The dust swirled up and she was overcome with a fit of sneezing and coughing.

"May I be of some assistance?"

The deep voice froze Cara. Her eyes swung to the trail, and through watery eyes she looked up at Lord Wilton astride his great black hunter. Viewing the twitch of humor around his mouth, Cara closed her eyes as if in pain. Summoning what dignity she could, she coolly faced him.

"Thank you, milord, but I'm fine now. Just a fit of sneezing." Valiantly Cara tried to look unconcerned at Julian's presence. "You may continue your ride," she encouraged him.

Her eyes flew open in terror as Julian threw his leg across the saddle and vaulted lightly to the ground. Like a child hoping to avoid discovery, she thrust the trap behind her back. For a moment she considered dropping to the ground in a fit of screaming hysteria. Why couldn't the blasted man just mind his own business? Through lowered eyes

107

she winced at the streaks of dirt on her dress. She was positive her face was as dust-covered as her hands. Out of the corner of her eye she spotted the rabbits and moved to cover them with the edge of her skirts. As Julian strode toward her, her heart bumped heavily inside her breast.

"Topping good day for a stroll, eh?"

Cara risked a glance up at Wilton's sun-bronzed face. As she felt the impact of his sharp brown eyes, she devoutly wished she had fallen into a swoon.

"Yes, Lord Wilton," Cara answered meekly. "I was just out for a bit of fresh air."

"I see, Miss Farraday," Julian drawled lazily. "And behind your back? Some wildflowers perhaps?"

She ground her teeth in frustration. Momentarily she debated holding her ground until he left. However, one look at the determined set of Julian's jaw disabused her of the idea that he might leave her in peace. Slowly, like a child presenting a surprise gift, Cara held out the cast-iron trap. At Julian's narrowed gaze, Cara found herself blushing in confusion.

"I—I tripped over it," she stammered.

Taking in the drops of blood on her skirt, Julian found his heart quickening in concern. He threw the trap to the ground, placing his hands on the embarrassed girl's shoulders.

"Are you hurt?" Julian's voice held a caressing tone as his hands massaged her shoulders.

As he tipped her face up toward his, a shiver coursed through Cara's body, and she felt the heat of his hands through the material of her dress.

"No. No. I just bruised my ankle," Cara exclaimed in a shaky voice. "It's really nothing."

"Let me have a look at it," Julian barked, kneeling on the leafy ground.

"Please, Lord Wilton. It's really fine." Cara's face flamed with embarrassment and mortification.

"Your foot, Miss Farraday, if you please."

Knowing there was no way to put off the inevitable, Cara cautiously raised the hem of her skirt. There, beside her feet, lay the bloodied bodies of the rabbits. Her humiliation was so great that she could only stare blankly at the trees in front of her.

"Busy day, Miss Farraday?" Julian asked teasingly.

A groan was her only answer. Silently Cara raised her injured foot for his inspection. Julian sucked in his breath as he noted the angry bruise on the swollen ankle. His fingers were gentle as he tested the bones for any further damage. Carefully he placed her foot on the ground and stood up, towering over the dainty governess.

"Come," he said gruffly. "Tyrr can carry us both."

"Thank you very much, Lord Wilton," Cara ground out in frustration. "But I would prefer walking. The exercise will keep my ankle from stiffening up."

Cara limped back to the path where the great hunter stood waiting. The horse tossed his head as Julian reached for the reins. He vaulted easily into the saddle, staring down at the disheveled girl beside the trail. Before she could protest further, he leaned sideways and scooped her up, placing her on the stallion in front of him.

"Miss Farraday, you are probably the most stubborn woman I have ever had the misfortune to come across." There was a trace of hurt puzzlement in his tone as he looked down at the girl. "You cannot find me so repulsive that you would refuse my assistance."

"It is not fitting, Lord Wilton," Cara answered primly.

Snorting in disgust at her missish ways, Julian nudged Tyrr into a gentle walk toward the Hall. Cara kept her backbone ramrod straight, avoiding as well as she could any contact with Julian. She dug her hands into Tyrr's mane to keep herself from bumping against her companion's chest, but remained agonizingly conscious of their intimate position. Each time her shoulder grazed his hard-muscled

109

body, Cara felt scorched by the heat. It took all of her willpower not to nestle into the curve of Julian's body, succumbing to the physical draw of his personality.

Wilton hummed tunelessly under his breath, apparently unaware of the turmoil going on in the girl. However, he, too, was conscious of the presence of tension between them. He was possessed with a maddening desire to crush the girl against his chest, caressing her until she relaxed unresistingly in his arms. Shaking his head to clear it of his lustful thoughts, Julian breathed in the fresh summer air. His brows drew down in bafflement and he inhaled again. Looking down at the girl holding herself so aloof, he took in again the bloodstains on her dress. As the smell of gin once again rose to assail his nostrils, Julian nodded in understanding.

"Your pardon, Miss Farraday, but do you generally start drinking gin so early in the day?"

Eyes flying open at the amused tone of voice, Cara summoned as much dignity as she could and finally snapped back her answer.

"I did not realize gin was forbidden to a governess, Lord Wilton."

Cara bristled at Julian's chuckle. Shortly the Hall came into sight, and she relaxed slightly, relieved that her forced proximity to her husband's disturbing presence would soon be at an end. Julian pulled Tyrr to a halt at the back entrance to the children's wing. Dismounting, he reached up and encircled Cara's waist, swinging her easily to the ground.

"May I suggest, Miss Farraday, that in the future you confine your walks to the paths rather than risk another bruised ankle."

With a gasp of outrage, Cara skewered Wilton with a flash of scorn. Flags of color flamed high on her cheeks as she drew herself erect. Julian thought she resembled nothing so much as a ruffled hen.

"And may I suggest, Lord Wilton, that in future you forbid the use of those poaching traps. Richard and Belin are always afoot in those woods, and it very well could have been one of them in the trap today." With that parting shot, Cara turned and limped into the Hall.

Damn the girl, Julian cursed as he leaped into the saddle. The unmitigated gall of the chit to chastise him for following the local practices. Angrily he drummed his heels into Tyrr's sides, and the startled horse snorted in annoyance.

As he raced up through the woods, Julian's anger abated, and he thought about the governess's last words. It was apparent from her begrimed appearance that she had helped someone out of the trap. It was immaterial who it had been. What mattered most to Julian was that it might very well have been Richard or Belin. The mere thought of the tiny girl with a leg mangled by the iron teeth of the trap gave Julian a queasy feeling in the pit of his stomach. It wouldn't hurt to put the word to Clemson, the gamekeeper, to dismantle the traps. As long as everyone believed they were still in use, they would act as a deterrent to poachers.

Julian puzzled over the perverse little governess as he rode back to the Hall. The duchess and his as yet unseen bride had definitely saddled him with a surprise package. He thought he had hired a passive, obedient servant, but the contrary wench turned into a fire breather whenever she was crossed. Perhaps if this trait had been used to benefit herself, Julian could more easily dismiss her from his mind. It appeared that the little American only fought in others' defense, never in her own. She was both intriguing and fascinating. He would definitely have to spend more time with the children in the schoolroom.

Cara was blissfully unaware of Julian's interest in her as she hobbled to her room. Muttering maledictions over her misfortune in running into Lord Wilton, she finally reached the safety of her room. When she glanced at herself in the mirror, she shuddered. What a hoyden Julian must think

111

her. She was forever covered with dirt, dust, or perspiration. He mingled with delicately scented, fragile ladies who combined beauty and grace to present a soothing picture. Every time she ran into him, she was positively filthy and presented the image of a viperous-tongued shrew.

"Miss Farraday?"

Hearing Richard's softly whispered voice, Cara scrubbed her face briskly and then crossed to let in the anxious boy.

"Will Pennyfeather be all right, Miss Farraday?" There was a slight quiver to the boy's chin, but he stared hopefully at his governess.

"Don't worry, Richard," Cara said, placing a steadying hand on his shoulder. "He'll be out after rabbits in no time at all."

"Topping good!" His face glowed with relief; then he flushed self-consciously as he remembered her own injuries. "And how is your ankle? I could get some liniment from Mrs. Clayton for you."

"I'd appreciate that, Richard. It's a bit sore, but I'm sure it will be fine by tomorrow."

Cara smiled as the boy scampered down the corridor, whistling happily now that all was right with his world. For the remainder of the evening Cara's ankle was propped up on pillows while the children entertained her. As she listened to the songs and the stories, her mind only occasionally wandered to a dark-haired man with brooding brown eyes.

Chapter Eight

"Stroke with your arms, Richard," Cara shouted to the boy thrashing wildly in the water. "That's right. Now you've got it."

Holding her skirt up out of the water, Cara leaned over and splashed cool water on her perspiring face. The hot, muggy summer day had only an occasional puffy cloud to obscure the punishing rays of the sun. Cara unbuttoned the collar of her dress and cursed the rough cotton material that clung in damp folds to her body. She knew Mrs. Clayton would scold her if the housekeeper saw her with the bright sun shining on her face. A lady of fashion was supposed to have skin the color of white magnolias. Fashion be hanged, Cara thought, relishing the heated warmth that invaded her body. She wriggled her toes ecstatically in the soft bottom of the lake.

Smiling, Cara shaded her eyes against the glare and watched Belin bounding up and down in the water. Lots of outside activities had done wonders for both Richard and Belin. They were thriving with the exercise and the fresh air. Cara's heart swelled with pride as she acknowledged the transformation that had taken place in the children. Belin was taking pride in her appearance, even though she had not given up many of her wilder ways. Richard had lost the unhealthy pallor, replaced by a hearty tan from his outdoor activities. His face no longer held its habitual withdrawn expression but was now more often wreathed in smiles.

"Watch, Miss Farraday," Richard shouted.

Applauding and laughing at the boy's antics, Cara's mind wandered to Julian. Much to the mystification of the household, he had begun a week of social calls, ostensibly to get better acquainted with the other landowners. From Glum, Cara learned the real reason behind the sudden flurry of visits. According to the worried head groom, Julian was hunting for the girl he had seen in the woods. For safety's sake, Cara had given up her morning ride and now chafed at the inactivity. Eventually he would lose interest, and then she could continue her riding.

As if she had conjured up the man, Cara sensed Julian's presence even before she actually saw him. Although he approached her and stood quietly beside her, she ignored him totally. Groaning inwardly at his intrusion, Cara fought to control the tranquil expression on her face. She concentrated determinedly on Richard as he swam haltingly across the water.

"Well done, Richard," Julian shouted to the puffing boy.

Startled by his uncle's unexpected presence, Richard gulped a mouthful of water and rose coughing in the waist-deep water. When Richard stopped choking, he stood red-faced, his expression setting in the sullen look that Cara dreaded. She waited breathlessly for Julian's caustic comment.

"How's the water, Belin?" Julian asked, ignoring the sulking boy. "Do you suppose I'd freeze to death if I came in?"

Richard stood transfixed, eyes widening in disbelief as Julian pulled off his boots and threw his jacket onto the sandy shore. Belin squealed with delight as her uncle's lithe body cut the water beside her. Julian swam out to the center of the lake, then turned and swam back to

114

stand beside his nephew, whose expression was one of dazed awe. Cara, as amazed as the children by the man's behavior, sank down on the towels with her back against a tree trunk. A smile of pure happiness flitted across her face as she watched Julian work with one child and then the other.

Her eyes roamed casually over the muscular body of the man who was, incredibly, her husband. His wet shirt clung to his chest, molding and rippling with his every move as he showed Richard how to stroke with his arms to best advantage. As her eyes dropped to the flat stomach and lean shanks of the man in the water, Cara blushed. She had to admit that Julian was a magnificent specimen, with the agile grace of a sleek animal. Leaning contentedly against the rough bark, Cara watched the frolics of the threesome in the water.

This was a totally different Julian. In her first interview with the man, he had been sarcastic, arrogant, and condescending. There was little evidence of these traits now as he played with the children. He was gentle but firm with Belin, coaxing her out into deeper water, then swooping her up in his arms when she faltered. Watching the adoration on Richard's face, Cara fervently prayed that this was not just a momentary whim of Julian's. The boy needed his guardian's companionship desperately, needed a person of his own class to act as role model. If only Julian's interest in the boy would last, Richard's life would be substantially more stable.

Conscious that Julian would safeguard the children, Cara's thoughts slipped backward in time to her own childhood. The summer had always been wonderful, full of long hours outside. Her parents had given her a great deal of freedom, she realized now, although at the time she took it all for granted. She swam and rode almost every day, falling asleep at night contented with her active days. One summer her father had tried to teach her to sail. Rigging a sail in a little dinghy, he stood on shore shouting instructions to her. But she was wholly inept, perhaps due to her lack of concentration and general joy in being on the water in any capacity.

"Those must be very happy thoughts."

At the sound of Julian's voice, Cara's eyes flew open to stare up at his towering figure. Automatically her hands flew to her headdress to be sure it was in place. Reassured, she sat up straighter and tucked her bare feet under the hem of her skirt.

"I was thinking about summer when I was a child," Cara answered softly.

"And was it a happy experience?" Julian asked, surprisingly interested in her reply.

"Yes," she purred contentedly. "Very."

Julian was touched by the wealth of emotion in such a few words. He threw himself down on the grass and studied the young woman with interest. Although she kept her eyes demurely cast down, Julian liked the feathery eyelashes that lay against her creamy skin. There was a spattering of freckles across the bridge of her nose that accentuated the youthful quality of the petite girl. By the rapid heartbeat visible on the side of her neck, Julian sensed that she was less than comfortable in his presence. But unlike most young women of his acquaintance, she did not chatter away her nervousness. Even though tense, there was a restful quality about her that bespoke a certain assurance of self.

"I have come to offer an apology, Miss Farraday."

"An apology? For what?" Cara asked in surprise.

"You were right to be angry with me. I was wholly ignorant about the children. And, being ignorant, I have done and said things that must have appeared needlessly cruel. Believe me, it was entirely unintentional."

From his tone of voice and the pained look on his face, Cara could not doubt the sincerity of his words. Her at-

116

titude toward him softened, but she was puzzled by his guilty admission. Noticing her bewilderment, Julian continued.

"It seems, Miss Farraday, that I must find out from others what I should have discovered for myself. In the last week I have had some very informative conversations with the members of my household. All of them, you may be assured, are singing your praises," Julian said, grinning when Cara squirmed at his compliment.

Sitting up, Julian wrapped his arms around his knees and looked out at the children playing in the water. He waved and smiled at the joyous shouts as they tried to outdo each other in performing for his approval. Sighing heavily, Julian turned once more to the pensive girl at his side.

"I was abroad when my brother died. It took some time for the news to reach me, and then I did not hurry home as perhaps I should have. My brother and I had been very close when we were growing up. We used to swim in this very spot. As the years passed, we grew apart. He was far too interested in women and gambling. Although I like both, for him it was not a hobby as much as it was an obsession."

Cara sat quietly with her hands folded in her lap, watching the play of emotion on Julian's face as he looked back in time. His voice held regret, sorrow, and resignation. It was obvious that his words covered a range of soul-searching. Cara remained still, not putting into words any thoughts of her own, only curious to hear the remainder of the story.

"I did not return for several months, and by that time the children were already installed in my home. I was a confirmed bachelor and will be honest confessing that I resented their presence in what had been a blissfully childless household. I absented myself as much as possible in the first year. Partly from having had little traffic with youngsters and, yes, I will have to admit it, from sheer lack of interest.''

At a shout from the water, Julian bounded up and shouted further instructions to Richard. Once this was well in train, he resumed his seat on the shore.

''I was aware of Belin's hands, but I had no idea how to deal with it. The only occasion when I could have said something to alleviate the child's embarrassment was ruined when the lady I was with screamed in fear at the sight of Belin's fingers. By the time I had calmed her, the child had fled, and I chose to ignore the situation.'' Julian spoke softly, sparing himself little in the telling of the incident.

''She seems to have come to terms with her hands,'' Cara said, briefly relating the story of the Frog Princess. ''Belin is convinced now that she is special rather than an oddity. As she grows older, she'll realize the story is merely a comfort to her, but by then she will have a stronger feeling of self-worth.''

Julian's eyes held approval as he listened to the young woman whose wisdom and common sense had quite literally transformed a wild child into a beautiful little wood nymph.

''If Belin continues as she is now, I am going to be besieged with offers from smitten young men.'' Julian laughed. Then, as his eyes swung out to the lake, his expression darkened. ''But with Richard I have no excuse except stupidity.''

Cara heard the note of pain in Julian's voice as he stared at the laughing boy in the water. Unconsciously, her hand reached out to touch him in reassurance, but she pulled it back quickly, embarrassed at her own forwardness.

''I didn't know Richard was with his parents in the carriage when it overturned.''

''Oh,'' breathed Cara in understanding. ''So, of course

you wouldn't know the reason behind his aversion to horses.''

"Exactly," Julian said approvingly, as though Cara were an exceptionally bright student. "His father was a superb horseman. I assumed Richard would be, too, and it would be a point of communication for us both. When he balked, I thought he was a coward. And, of course, he knew what I was thinking, but was apparently too proud to admit the reason for his fear. I tore into him, I'm afraid, but the lad is pluck to the bone and held his ground. I should have been horsewhipped."

They sat in silence, both sets of eyes on the water, lost in thought. Suddenly Julian burst out laughing, throwing his head back in helpless amusement. Startled, Cara stared at the shaking figure as though he had taken leave of his senses.

"If you had been a proper young English woman, you would certainly have jumped to my defense," Julian managed to get out when he could control his laughter.

"Well, perhaps horsewhipping would have been a little strong," Cara stammered in confusion.

"Caning, possibly?" Julian offered. As Cara appeared to be considering the idea, Julian laughed again. "Are all Americans without artifice, or are you a particularly prickly and honest one?"

"I am a very normal person, I assure you," Cara defended primly. "As the children's governess, perhaps I do judge you more severely. If so, I apologize."

"I meant no offense, Miss Farraday," Julian replied solemnly, but his eyes were sparkling with mischief. "Are you enjoying your position here at Weathersfield?"

"Yes, of course, Lord Wilton," Cara replied demurely. "I am very fond of the children."

Julian noted the genuine sincerity of her words as she gazed at the capering youngsters. He knew without being told that Miss Farraday had come to love both Belin and

119

Richard. Perhaps that was why she had been so successful in dealing with them. Now that he was able to examine them with more interest, he was finding them quite fascinating himself.

Cara sensed the brush of Julian's glance and felt her cheeks redden under his close scrutiny. She had not minded listening to his admissions of past dealings with the children. She had merely been a sounding board for his thoughts. But now that the conversation was no longer about the children and her duties as governess, she was uncomfortable. Fearing the personal nature of further discussion, Cara stood up quickly, shaking her skirts out as she walked toward the edge of the lake.

Julian admired the unconscious grace of Cara's movements, and catching sight of the bare feet peeking out of the bottom of her skirts, he smiled broadly. Glancing at her dress, he felt an impatience with the frumpy design. She looks as if she's borrowed the dress from an older and evidently larger sister, he thought. Her limp headdress gave her the appearance of a young nun. Now that Julian was used to the dowdy style of her clothing, he was also more aware of the figure beneath the bulky materials. To his discerning eye, the mysterious Miss Farraday had a petite but delightfully curved body.

Reminding himself bleakly of his married state, Julian shook himself to clear his mind of an inventory of the governess's physical attributes and watched as she dealt with the children. Cajoling them out of the water with a combination of humor and outrageous threats, Cara amazed him with the respect for her authority she had already instilled in the children. They responded quickly and eagerly to her orders, behaving neither sullenly nor toadylike. Thoughtfully, Julian retrieved his boots and jacket. Waving and calling his good-byes, he strolled to his horse, tethered to a nearby bush.

The children were slightly downcast by Julian's abrupt

departure, but Cara was relieved. Replacing her stockings and half boots, she praised both of them lavishly on their progress in the water. By the time the children were reasonably dry, Belin was once again chattering and Richard was badgering Cara with more questions about the Indians, a subject that consumed the greater part of his interest in the Americas.

After their morning of exercise, the children fell on the food at lunch with great enthusiasm. Cara was delighted with the boisterous discussions of the children, remembering only too well the halting conversations at the beginning of her stay. She realized that her days as governess would quickly end. Another week and a half at most, she thought, surprised at the jolt of disappointment she felt. Perhaps she was enjoying herself so much because she was free of all responsibility except for the well-being of the children. On her marital responsibilities she would rather not dwell.

When the luncheon was finished, Cara sent Belin to Mrs. Clayton for her needlework lesson. Cautiously she eyed Richard, who was engrossed in reading a history book. His shaggy curls were mussed as he occasionally ran a hand absently through them. Cara bit her lip in perturbation, opening her mouth several times in an attempt to speak, then snapping her lips shut in indecision. She wondered if she were pushing Richard too quickly. There was so little time left that she felt pressured at least to make an attempt. After all, the boy could only refuse, and then she would just have to try a new tack.

"Richard?" Cara began nervously.

"Yes, Miss Farraday."

Looking up from the book he was reading, Richard put a finger between the pages to save his place. He waited patiently as his governess hesitated in phrasing her words.

"I wonder if you could help me?"

"If I can," the boy replied politely.

Cara cleared her throat self-consciously before she could continue. "I talked to Glum yesterday, and he said he thought I ought to ride again."

The tensing of the boy's hands on the edges of the book were the only visible sign of his uneasiness. Ashamed of her own subterfuge, Cara flushed with discomfort and threw herself into a chair across from the boy.

"I can't do it alone," she blurted out. "Could you come with me?" she finished lamely. She wrung her hands nervously, anguished to think that all the planning she and Glum had done might be for nothing.

Mistaking her discomposure for fear, Richard leaped to his feet. He threw down the book and stood manfully in front of her, a slim, blushing protector.

"Of course I'll come, Miss Farraday," he chivalrously announced to the startled woman. Then continuing in a surprisingly adult tone, he said, "I've been wanting to suggest it, but I wasn't sure if I . . . I mean, if you were ready."

The boy was delighted by the ravishing smile his governess bestowed on him. For one awkward moment he almost thought she was going to hug him. On his way to his room he reflected that it might not be such an awful thing if Miss Farraday did. At first her looks had been rather offputting, but now that he knew her better, he rather thought she had moments when she was downright pretty. He was glad she hadn't gone all mushy like a lot of ladies he had met. After all, a fellow of his years didn't relish being pawed over by some overly scented lady. Of course that couldn't really apply to Miss Farraday. He had noticed early on that she smelled like a garden in summer. Lots of clean smells, with a little bit of spice, he thought. Putting the finishing touches to his riding habit, he acknowledged that Miss Farraday was a right one, as Pennyfeather would say.

After Richard left, Cara flew to the bell rope and then

hastily scribbled a note to Glum apprising him of Richard's consent. She was excited beyond belief as she hurried to change her clothes. After nearly being caught by Julian, she had abandoned the dove-gray habit, and choosing one of the dismal brown tweed dresses in her meager wardrobe, she had resewn it for riding. She made a wry face as she stared at her reflection in the mirror; the dress was far from flattering, bunching around her waist like a sack. The color vied with the natural beauty of her skin, giving it a slightly yellow cast. Checking her hair to be certain that it was securely pinned at the nape of her neck, she covered it with an equally unbecoming tweed headdress. Rapidly she pulled on her riding boots and raced down the stairs to the stables.

Richard was waiting in the stable yard, nervously swatting his crop against a bush. Although he would never admit it, Cara sensed his agitation. Hoping to give the boy confidence, she put on her most timorous expression as she approached.

"Are you ready?" Cara asked in feigned quavering tones.

"Don't worry, Miss Farraday." Richard spoke heartily. "I asked Glum to find the gentlest horse in the stables."

"I don't know. Do you suppose if I breathe deeply, it will help to get rid of the butterflies in my stomach?"

"A jolly good idea," Richard exclaimed, immediately trying it. "It really works, Miss Farraday. Give it a go."

Cara watched apprehensively as Glum came out into the yard. He was walking the docile hunter they had picked out for Richard. An older horse, Grady, was placid to the point of somnolence, a nerveless animal who promised to give Richard an uneventful ride. One of the boys walked behind Glum leading Rose, an unprepossessing mare, for Cara. While she dithered needlessly, Richard was mounted with no hesitation on his part. The boy was far too busy shouting instructions to his hapless and apparently inept governess to be concerned about his own fear. Cara was just reaching for the saddle when a voice behind her caused her to falter in consternation.

"Good afternoon, Richard. Are you on your way out?"

"Yes, Uncle Julian," the boy replied, grinning at Cara's disconcerted expression. "Miss Farraday is going to have her first ride in ever so long a time. I'm going to go with her to give her encouragement."

The alarm on Glum's face was equally reflected on Cara's. If ever there was a time that she would have wished Julian elsewhere, it was now. Would he recognize her as the girl he had seen in the woods? It took all of Cara's willpower to stand quietly beside the gentle mare and not bolt for the Hall.

"I've already been out, but perhaps she would feel braver if I went along," Julian offered, misinterpreting the fear evident on the girl's face.

Beside her, Glum groaned, and Cara closed her eyes to prevent herself from screaming in frustration. Momentarily she debated abandoning the entire plan. She could plead illness or insanity. Anything to get out of the yard and back to the safety of the Hall. Then her eyes flicked to Richard's ecstatic expression, and she sighed in resignation.

"Oh, topping, Uncle Julian. Right, Miss Farraday?" Richard chirped, unaware of his governess's discomfort in the presence of his guardian.

"Topping, indeed, Richard," Cara echoed dryly.

Catching Julian's look of cool amusement, angry color flushed her cheeks. She had an uncontrollable urge to throw something at her husband as he sat grinning astride the restive Tyrr. Knowing she was only prolonging the inevitable, she got ready to mount, of necessity prepared to act the part of a totally inexperienced rider.

Gritting her teeth, she purposely approached the horse from the wrong side. When the mare shied away, Cara righted herself, and hauling on the reins, she moved determinedly to the mounting block. As ungracefully as possible she flung herself on the saddle, bunching the riding skirt around her legs and tangling it in the stirrup. Glum, his wizened face red and perspiring, refused to meet her eyes as she fussed with her skirt, knotted the reins, and clumsily dropped her riding crop. Both Julian and Richard waited stoically through all the confusion. They exchanged sympathetic glances, acknowledging the imcompetence of women. When Cara announced she was ready, the two males sighed heavily in accord.

Despite her own discomfort, Cara's heart sang at Richard's behavior. Urging his governess forward, the boy praised her lavishly, if unfoundedly. He was too busy shouting instructions to her to be at all concerned about himself. Richard sat his horse as though he had never felt any trepidation about riding. Caught up in the glorious excitement of the moment, he soon forgot that his prime objective was to give Miss Farraday encouragement. Followed closely by Julian, Richard set a brisk pace along the track. Cara was left to her own devices and trailed miserably after them.

Riding hunched over to look as awkward as possible, Cara cursed again at the picture she made. From the pained contemplation under scowling black brows, Julian was apparently convinced of her performance as an inadequate horsewoman. Despite the fact that this was exactly what Cara had intended, she was furious at this easy acceptance of this fact. It was true that she did not want him to recognize her as the girl on the dainty gray mare, but on the other hand, she would have preferred that he not see her ungainly manner on this lumbering excuse for a horse. When Julian turned in his saddle to check on her progress, she deliberately kneed the mare off the trail, flapping the reins ineffectually.

"In some difficulty?" Julian asked in amusement as he

grasped her lead rein. Bringing the mare's head around and directing it along the path, Julian fell in beside her.

Astride the beautiful black Tyrr, he dwarfed Cara on the inelegantly plodding mare. Julian appeared to great advantage on the back of a horse. His bronzed skin glowed with health, and his dark curls shimmered in the sunlight. Cara's eyes scanned his muscled torso, approving the strength apparent beneath his buckskins. A blush suffused her neck and face as she forced here eyes away from his body. In her confusion she fumbled the reins, nearly dropping them, and winced at the pity on Julian's face.

"I had no idea you were so inept at riding, Miss Farraday," Julian teased. "From what Glum told me of your plan for Richard, I did not realize that you could barely keep your seat."

"I was not hired as a riding instructor, Lord Wilton," Cara ground out stiffly, unable to hide the irritation in her voice.

"It is impolite of me to twit you with your inability to ride," Julian apologized, but the sparkle of laughter behind his eyes did little to improve Cara's temper. "I thought by joining you this afternoon, I might be of some help. However, if I had known sooner, I could have saved you discomfort by taking Richard out myself."

"I applaud your motives, but you see, Lord Wilton, the whole idea was to get Richard to stop worrying about himself. And that, you will have to admit, has been possible by my very ineptness."

Together, their eyes followed the boy who was happily unconscious that he was the subject of their discussion. Swatting occasionally at the bushes beside the trail, the boy forged ahead, at ease in the saddle, all fear forgotten. Julian's warm brown eyes swung to hers, and he touched his gloved hand to his hat in a victory salute. Spurring his horse, he joined his nephew and began to point out various objects in the woods.

For Cara the ride was endless. Finally it was Julian who suggested that Miss Farraday might like to return to the Hall. Thus reminded of his duty to his governess, Richard was most solicitous of Cara on the return trip. His fear of horses might never have existed. How resilient children were, she thought gratefully. From the moment Richard had mounted the hunter, that frightened period of his life was erased completely.

Back in the stable yard, Glum paced anxiously, waiting for a glimpse of the returning threesome. He bounded eagerly forward to help Cara dismount. In her effort once again to appear graceless, she almost tumbled to the ground atop the panting head groom. Richard tried valiantly to smother his snort of amusement. Cara glared at the boy and then cast a withering glance at Julian, who was grinning like the village idiot. Stiff-legged with affronted pride, she stalked off in the direction of the Hall, while behind her she could hear Richard gleefully accepting Julian's offer to ride the next day.

Safe in her room, Cara collapsed on the bed. A great upsurge of relief washed over her as she remembered the success of her plan. Despite her chagrin at Julian's presence, she had to admit that his being there had made the outing much more special for Richard. It easily paved the way for other rides and a continued communication between the boy and his guardian. Cara knew that Richard desperately needed his uncle's approbation to build up his self-esteem. He was surrounded by women in the household and needed to see a masculine point of view to grow into the kind of man Cara would wish him to be. She was contented that the relationship between the man and the boy was burgeoning.

Glaring at the ugly riding habit lying on the floor as she soaked in the tub, Cara promised she would burn it at her first opportunity. Closing her eyes, she could picture laughing brown eyes in a bronzed face. Just once, she thought wistfully, I wish that Julian could see me as I truly am instead of as an awkward or cantankerous girl. She had always felt herself to be poised and socially adept. But in Julian's presence she reverted to a graceless gawk of a schoolgirl. Writhing in embarrassment, she recalled each of her encounters with her husband. Finally, in resignation, she sat up briskly and sponged herself clean.

Chapter Nine

To Cara's chagrin, in the days that followed Julian took an increasing interest in the children. It was not unusual for Cara to glance up from her schoolbooks to find the disconcerting brown eyes spearing her from the doorway. More and more often, Julian found excuses to pass the schoolroom or to check with Richard about the time for their ride. Belin and Richard fought to outdo each other in inventing reasons that he should stay to hear their lessons. The children were overjoyed when their guardian acceded to their badgering, but Cara was less than enthused.

Cara noticed that Richard, in particular, was thriving under the attention from his uncle. The sullen, taciturn young man became as happily talkative as Belin. His eyes glowed with pride, and he vied with his sister in showing off before their guardian. When Julian arrived, the lessons were disrupted while he launched into a description of his adventures abroad. Richard, eyes filled with hero worship, bombarded the older man with questions, his inquisitive mind titillated by the narratives of new worlds.

At these times Cara attempted to remain in the background. She sat in the window alcove embroidering, hoping not to attract Julian's attention, Her eyes covertly watched the expressions flitting across his face as he described strange sights and wild and, she suspected, largely fictitious dangers. His efforts to please the children endeared him to her as no other action could have.

For his part, Julian genuinely enjoyed his hours in the schoolroom. The clamor of the children and the delightful homeyness of the room were a solace; he had been without family for a majority of his life. It brought back to him the happy days of his own childhood, when he and his brother heartily threw themselves into the caprices of early boyhood. He was delighted to find that Richard was so much like his father. The boy had a great curiosity about the workings of the world and a penchant for mischief. Slowly Julian was getting acquainted with his nephew and finding a pleasure in his company. Even Belin was beginning to take on the qualities of a young lady.

However, much to Julian's annoyance, he discovered it was Miss Farraday who was the magnet that drew him to the schoolroom. He was honest enough to admit that if he only wanted to see the children, he could send for them at will. The one time that he had done that, the little governess had absented herself. So, in confusion, Julian sought her out in the schoolroom.

The redoubtable Miss Farraday was certainly a puzzle. It had not been a month since she had taken his household by storm. He could recall her apparently shy and docile nature. He should have been forewarned when she almost lost her temper at that first interview. The servants could not say or do enough for her; the children patently adored her. He watched in amazement her handling of his niece and nephew. She treated them as reasonable human beings, listening to their statements with an open-minded interest that, to Julian's mind, was totally ungovernesslike. Despite her own youth, she seemed to have a finely tuned intuition of when to be firm and when a subtle diplomacy was needed. Her quiet presence was restful, and yet Julian could recall instances where the passionate anger that bristled beneath her acquiescent manner had broken loose. She was at once a nonentity and an enigma.

"And why do I care?" Julian muttered under his breath. He was sitting on the floor building a castle of blocks with the children. His eyes darted to the window seat, where Miss Farraday was sewing. You are a married man, his mind accused. What do you want from the girl?

Julian shook his head in confusion. He didn't know what he wanted. The little American was in his thoughts constantly. When he didn't see her during the day, his feet brought him willy-nilly to the door of the schoolroom. For now, all he wanted was to be in her presence. But he realized angrily that beneath the surface there was a rolling wave of desire that threatened to overcome his better nature. Just staring at the girl, he could feel the tightness gathering in his loins.

Julian's ever watchful eyes caught the glimmer of a smile on Cara's face, and he wondered what had caused such a contented expression. In a burst of anger he considered the fact that she might have found a suitor among his household staff or his tenants. He hoped that none of the men would importune the girl, whose youth would be very tempting to someone of jaded appetite. The scandal of the last governess had been narrowly averted, and Julian would never permit a recurrence. Of course, that young lady's story had been that Edward Tallworth had seduced her; however, her avaricious demands made it difficult to believe that she was less than a willing partner to the seduction.

Perhaps I ought to warn Miss Farraday about Tallworth, Julian considered. Sort of give her a little fatherly advice.

He snorted in disgust thinking about the man. It had been a peaceful ten days since Tallworth had gone north on business. He was due back shortly, and Julian hoped his interest in Miss Farraday had diminished. For all her maturity with the children, the little American appeared unaware of the dangers inherent in her position.

"Would you, Uncle Julian?"

Richard's voice broke into Julian's reverie. He blinked his eyes several times until he could focus on the boy sitting beside him on the floor.

"I'm sorry, lad. I'm afraid I wasn't attending," Julian muttered, uncomfortably aware that his nephew had been speaking to him before he became so mired in his own thoughts.

"I asked if you'd like to see Loki?" the boy repeated patiently.

"And what, pray tell, is a loki?" Julian asked with a smile.

"It's not an it. It's a him." Then, tired of the word game, he burst out, "it's the colt that Miss Farraday and I have been taking care of."

"I see. Well, in that case, I would be delighted to see him."

Leaving Belin in the kitchen, where she could be cosseted with cookies and sticky buns, Cara followed Julian and Richard to the stables. The boy could barely contain his excitement, skipping ahead and then dashing back to exhort them to greater speed. They gathered up Glum as they entered the stables, and their footsteps echoed on the wooden floors as they approached Loki's stall.

"He's still pretty small, Uncle Julian," Richard stated defensively as he prepared to open the door of the box. "But I just know he's going to be a smashing good horse."

"Well, let's have a look at him." Julian stood back so that the nervous boy could lead the slim-legged animal out into the main part of the stable.

Cara and Glum hung back, giving the lad room to shine. They held their breaths, eyes riveted on Julian's expressionless face. The black-browed man stood motionless, eyeing the colt through narrowed eyes. Richard's hands shook on the lead rope, but he remained silent while his uncle inspected his prize. Slowly Julian paced around the young stallion. With gentle hands he stroked the horse, testing the muscles and verifying the satiny coat and well-brushed mane.

"I think you may be right, Richard," Julian agreed.

"Thank you, sir." Richard wriggled in ecstasy at his guardian's approval.

"He does appear to be an exceptionally fine specimen. Obviously he should only be sold to the finest rider. Someone who can appreciate his qualities."

"Sold?" The boy gulped in fear. He moved protectively to Loki, stroking his forelock as the horse nuzzled his chest.

"Yes, But of course we would be careful whom he went to. No bruising rider or cow-handed neophyte."

"Oh, Uncle Julian, you really wouldn't sell him, would you?"

Julian almost smiled at the heartbreak in the voice of his nephew but held his mouth steady as he tilted his head to the side, staring intently at the colt.

"You might be right, halfling. It wouldn't be fitting to sell such a fine animal." The boy slumped in relief, then stiffened as Julian continued. "He ought to be given to someone who would have sense enough to take care of such a magnificent horse. Do you think you would be able to take care of him, lad?"

The last words were spoken so softly and so unexpectedly that at first the boy was not sure that he had heard correctly. Then, in comprehension, his face whitened, and his eyes lifted to Julian's for confirmation of the gift. At his uncle's answering nod, Richard gasped and in a flash of motion hurled himself on the older man.

Cara's vision was blurred with tears as she fumbled her

way out into the stable yard. Beside her, Glum blew his nose noisily into a voluminous handkerchief, then spat into the dust. Sheepishly they grinned at each other, content to have witnessed the growing trust between the boy and his uncle. Cara's steps were light on the way back to the Hall, but she halted abruptly when she saw Edward Tallworth walking jauntily toward her.

"Good afternoon, Miss Farraday," Tallworth called, making an exaggeratedly mocking leg.

"Sir Edward," Cara acknowledged coolly as she continued on the path. Her heart fluttered anxiously as she caught the calculating gleam in Tallworth's eye.

"Is it too much to hope that you have missed me?" he asked as they drew abreast.

"I am afraid, Sir Edward, that I was not aware that you were away." Cara lied without a qualm. She had been relieved at his absence since the night he had accosted her in the garden.

"And how are your charges?" he asked unctuously.

"Doing well, thank you. In fact, you must excuse me, for I am late for Belin's lessons."

For a moment Cara thought Tallworth would attempt to bar her way. But as he reached out an arm to detain her, his eyes flicked over her shoulder and he immediately dropped the hand to his side. Hearing Richard's and Julian's voices as they approached along the path, Cara quickly skirted around Tallworth and hurried to the safety of the Hall.

Cara crouched before the fireplace, blowing determinedly on the dying fire. A flame flicked out, curling around one of the small pieces of kindling she had just added. She blew once, and the flame disappeared; then, as she continued blowing, it flared out stronger, finally catching on the tinder. Despite the heat of the day, Cara relished her fire at night to combat the slight chill from the exterior stone walls. She frowned in annoyance at the fire. She had been reading and had let it get too low. After a few more pokings and proddings, the fire crackled briskly, and she curled up in a chair with her book. Her eyes stared at the pages, but her mind was far away, unable to comprehend the words she saw. Her time at Weathersfield was almost up. She could expect a summons from her grandmother to end the masquerade at any time. When she had begun the charade, she had planned to be merely an observer. It was evident that her character did not permit such a passive role. She had hurled herself into the affairs of the children, confronting Julian when she felt he was in the wrong. It seemed she made a very poor employee. Not only did she become totally involved with her charges but she had also fallen in love with her employer.

Soon she would go back to her grandmother's and resume the role of Caroline Leland, young lady of fashion and bride of Julian, Lord Wilton.

For the hundredth time Cara wondered if Julian would recognize her. She hoped, with proper clothing and with her red-gold hair curling softly around her face, she would be a far cry from the dowdy governess. She wondered how he would deal with her. Would he take the time to get to know his bride? She did not know what Julian expected from their relationship. He had agreed to the marriage, but would it be in name only? How could she explain to him that she already loved him, and she was prepared to be more than just the mother of his heir? This thought brought the blood rushing to her cheeks, and she hurriedly turned her mind into safer channels.

The candles flickered on the table beside her at the opening of the schoolroom door.

Edward Tallworth lounged in the doorway, a smug, satisfied smile on his face. The silence in the room and in the rest of the Hall made Cara conscious of the lateness of the hour and the inappropriateness of his visit.

"May I help you?" Cara asked coldly.

At Tallworth's leering expression, Cara hastily rose from her chair. Even standing, she felt at a disadvantage as the man loomed ominously in the doorway. It had never occurred to her that she might be in danger in her own rooms. There was an air of menace around Tallworth that had frightened Cara in the garden, but now it was even more powerful. Although her nervousness had increased at the silence of the figure in the doorway, she tried to keep her voice even and unemotional.

"I suggest you see me in the morning, Sir Edward, if you have a question for me." Her tone was dismissive, but Tallworth made no move to leave.

"Thought we ought to get better acquainted. After all, I am the children's uncle, and I like to keep appraised of their progress."

Tallworth entered the room, closing the door behind him. Although no expression crossed Cara's face, she felt a jolt of fear along her spine. Her eyes darted to her bedroom door, and she debated whether she should make a break for it or hold her ground. Her heart hammered painfully, filling her ears with the sound. Her lips trembled, and she had to moisten them before she was able to speak.

"I'm very sorry, Sir Edward, but it's late and I am extremely tired. We'll have to continue this conversation in the morning. I'm afraid it would be hardly suitable at this hour."

She had tried to speak crisply, but her voice quivered slightly with the fear engendered by the presence of the man. She felt trapped, wanting to run but afraid that any overt action would trigger immediate violence in the tense figure across the room. Her eyes began to search the room for a weapon, even as she realized that shortly she would need to be able to defend herself.

"Please call me Edward, Miss Farraday." His tongue had trouble with the syllables of her name, indicating that he had been drinking heavily most of the evening.

"If you will please leave, Sir Edward, we can talk at another time." As she spoke, Cara was edging closer to the door of her room, but Tallworth had already ascertained her direction and effectively cut her off.

"After all, Miss Farraday," Tallworth continued as though she had not spoken, "you have been here almost a month, and I feel we should be able to work out a closer relationship."

"I can see no possible reason that we should have any relationship at all," Cara snapped in anger. Although she managed to speak bravely, her whole body began to tremble.

"Despite your pathetic wardrobe, I feel you have great potential." Tallworth leered at her, leaving little to her imagination as to his intentions. As he spoke, he staggered toward her, devouring her with his eyes.

"I beg your pardon, sir."

Cara was terrified now but tried desperately to portray dignified outrage. She knew instinctively that if she showed her fear, he would cease the cat-and-mouse game and pounce on her immediately. All she could hope for was to play for time, trusting to chance for an opportunity to outwit his attack. As he circled around the chair toward her, she tried a bold manuever.

"I can no longer remain in this room when you insult me."

With racing heart Cara stalked toward the door in the corridor. Her movement caught him by surprise and for a moment she thought she might actually be able to escape. As Tallworth's look of surprise turned to fury, he charged after her, grabbing her arm and pulling her toward him.

Cara struggled but was afraid of precipitating anything worse.

"You're hurting my arm," Cara cried, her voice shaking with a combination of anger and hysteria.

"Now, my dear, pray give over the coy maidenly act. I'm sure we can come to some agreement."

Tallworth spun her around, and his lips swooped down to capture hers in a punishing kiss. His liquor-laden breath gagged her as she struggled ineffectually within the embrace. As his kiss deepened, Cara began to struggle in earnest, fighting down her panic and rising faintness. Loosing one of her hands, she swung and caught him heavily on the ear. As he staggered away, she broke loose and ran toward her bedroom door. Her hand touched the knob, but with a leap, Tallworth was on her before she could gain entrance. She winced in pain as he threw her against the door, reaching for her feverishly.

"For that, my dear, you will pay dearly," Tallworth snarled gutturally.

Cara cried out before he could kiss her again and, raising her foot, kicked him in the leg. Her soft slippers made little dent in his leather boots. An evil smile lit Tallworth's face as he pulled her inexorably toward him. She moaned in fear and pain as his grasping fingers bit into her shoulders.

"Excuse me, Edward. I am sure you can find entertainment elsewhere."

Julian's ice-tinged voice was startling in the stillness of the room. Tallworth's grip loosened, and Cara staggered back against the wall. Shaking with relief, she was unable to make a sound as she fought to catch her breath.

Julian's eyes blazed with anger as he watched the girl fighting for self-possession. He was startled by the purity of the lines of her face, seen in the shimmering light of the fire. Her blue-green eyes were dilated, a glowing counterpoint to the whiteness of her skin. Staring into the luminescent face of the frightened girl, he ached for the wounded vulnerability he saw etched on her soul. His eyes swung to the discomposed Tallworth, and it was all that he could do not to bolt across the room and beat the man into insensibility for causing this innocent even one moment of pain or discomfort. He had always thought that Tallworth was contemptible and blamed himself for permitting the man anywhere near Miss Farraday. With the man's unsavory history, the girl should have been protected from this sort of savagery.

Shaken by Tallworth's aborted attack and Julian's providential arrival, Cara could only stare mutely at her rescuer. She watched the mix of emotions mirrored in his eyes. Concern for her, anger at Tallworth, and another more intangible expression that Cara could not put a name to. Unable to voice her appreciation and aware that once more Julian had found her in another untenable position, a blush of color swept up her throat, and with a swirl of skirts, she threw open the door of her room. Inside, she leaned weakly against the wood and shot the bolt for additional safety.

The soft crackling of the fire was the only sound in the schoolroom as Julian flung a blazing scowl at Tallworth, who was rearranging his clothing in unconcern. The muscles of one of Julian's eyes twitched as he fought to control his temper. "After Miss Corday's precipitous departure," Julian remarked coldly, "I would have thought you would confine your dalliances to somewhere other than the schoolroom."

"I feel your arrival was less than welcome, Julian," Tallworth bluffed, nonchalantly retying his cravat with the utmost care.

"Let me make myself perfectly clear. Governesses are very difficult to find. I do not enjoy interviewing a new one every few months. I will not have you taking advantage of this one.'' Julian bit off his words sharply in sur-pressed fury.

"Hah! Taking advantage, indeed,'' Tallworth snarled back. "I would say the reverse was more likely. The chit was waiting for me in the corridor.''

For some reason this statement ripped away the last vestiges of Julian's control, and he grasped Tallworth by his newly tied cravat, almost lifting him from the floor.

"I don't care if she comes to you without a stitch on. If you touch her again, I will break every bone in your body.''

The quietly spoken words were all the more threatening. Shrugging off Julian's hands, Tallworth straightened his neckcloth. His facial expression mirrored a trace of fear, along with a decidedly calculating leer. Squaring his shoulders, he strolled toward the door, uncomfortably conscious of Julian's eyes boring into his back.

"If you wanted her for yourself, old boy, you only had to tell me,'' Tallworth drawled as he disappeared through the door into the corridor.

Julian stood rooted to the floor, clenching and unclenching his hands. He wanted desperately to tear after the other man and smash his fists into Tallworth's smirking face. He literally trembled with emotion as he fought to control his rage. Blindly he turned toward Cara's door, wanting to assure her that she was no longer in danger. He would offer his protection for as long as she needed it. He would hold her in his arms and promise to keep her safe from harm.

"Damn,'' Julian swore, turning away from the bedroom door. Storming down the corridor, he wondered at his own innocence where Miss Farraday was concerned. He was a married man and could offer neither protection nor sanctuary to the little governess. Is that what he wanted to give the girl, or was he as guilty as Tallworth in wanting only to caress the lithe body beneath the

140

dowdy clothes? His mind conjured up a picture of the girl spread naked in front of the fire, skin glowing in the flickering light. Groaning, Julian slammed into the library. He reached blindly for the decanter of brandy. Hurling himself into a chair, he poured a liberal portion into a glass and downed it quickly.

It was obvious that Tallworth would have to leave Weathersfield. The man had imbibed for the better part of the evening. Julian had watched him warily, knowing that his debauched habits and continued interest in the little governess would eventually lead to trouble. When Tallworth disappeared, Julian knew without conscious thought that he would find him in the schoolroom.

"It will give me the greatest pleasure to throw the bastard out!" Julian snarled, pouring another glassful of brandy.

After she bolted the door, Cara's knees gave out, and she sank to the floor beside the bed. Her whole body shook in relief at her narrow escape. Eventually her trembling gave way to a bone-jarring anger.

"How dare that man touch me?" Cara raged.

She had done absolutely nothing to encourage Tallworth. He had merely attacked her for his own sexual gratification. She ground her teeth, remembering how casually he had appraised her body and how he had taken it for granted that she would not only accept his advances but welcome them.

Having been raised in a sheltered environment, Cara was unprepared for the realities of an unprotected female's life. In dawning awareness she wondered if other female servants were the object of the lustful advances of their employers. It was only now that she realized the true dangers of her situation. As a member of the gentry, she had always been safe in the company of gentlemen. She had been chaperoned in public, but the idea that she might be subject to an attack on her person in private was inconceivable.

She wondered in confusion if her grandmother could have any conception of her vulnerability. Cara doubted it, for if she had, her grandmother would never have countenanced this masquerade.

Tiredly Cara stood up and staggered toward the washstand. She poured water into the basin with trembling hands. Stripping off her clothes, she scrubbed her body until her skin reddened, and still she felt violated by Tallworth's touch. Her teeth chattered convulsively as she curled up into a tight ball beneath the covers. Slowly, as warmth began to creep into her body, she relaxed and fell asleep.

Chapter Ten

Despite her nightmare-broken sleep, Cara was up before dawn. She lay wide-eyed in the feather bed, watching as the first rosy tint of light fell on the silk wallpaper of her room. Her body felt logy; her mind whirled with uneasy and half-thought ideas. Her first instinct was to escape back to the safety of her grandmother's presence. Tallworth's attack had disoriented her, shaking the foundation of security she had held to be an inviolable part of herself. Up to now her life had been a sheltered one, she realized. She had never been in physical want for any of the basic needs, never had to call on her own character strengths before, never been really tested.

Cara had known sorrow at the death of her mother, and then more recently with her father's death. She had felt frustration with the marriage that had been arranged for her. She had felt anger and the burgeoning of passion in her relationship with Julian. But she had never known fear. The attack in the schoolroom had frightened her out of all proportion to any other emotion. But with that fear came a realization of her own inner strength. She did not have to run away; she would stay until her grandmother sent for her. With that resolution made, Cara jumped out of bed to don her riding habit.

Since Julian had been riding with Richard most days,

Cara had been able to resume her morning rides in safety. Although Glum had told her that Julian had not been going out in the early mornings, she still avoided the jumps in the high meadows, content to roam the countryside and enjoy the woods. When he observed the haunted circles beneath her eyes, Glum shook his head in worry but threw her up onto Gentian's back without comment.

As the horse paced slowly uphill, Cara unpinned her hair from the confining bun and swung it loosely back over her shoulders. She emitted a purr of contentment as the morning sun beamed through the trees, falling on her upturned face. Freeing a hand from the reins, she stretched along Gentian's neck, patting and crooning to the graceful little mare.

The woods thinned and Cara drew rein, listening to the early morning sounds. Summer was in full bloom in England; the fields and hedgerows were a blaze of color. Walking the mare slowly to the edge of the woods, Cara looked down the hillside to the estate spread out below her. From this height she could make out the gentle roll of hills that led down to the lake and the outbuildings behind the massive edifice of Weathersfield Hall. Her eyes kindled with a glow of pleasure as she was able to pick out the familiar places she had visited.

It was strange to think back a month, when she had first come to Weathersfield. Then the sheer size of the Hall had overwhelmed her. She thought she would never be able to feel comfortable within the great stone dwelling. The children had been instrumental in making her feel at home. To them the Hall had been no more intimidating than a smaller place. They seemed to understand intuitively that a household was filled with people, and that was what mattered. Cara had found welcome and friendship with the servants and the tenants. She had met them and lived with them in the inconspicuous role of governess, so they had been open with her in a way that would never have been possible if she had first come to Weathersfield as Julian's bride.

When she returned, her welcome would be different. It saddened Cara to realize that when she returned as Lady Wilton, the open relationship would be gone, superseded by a respect for her position and a sense of propriety that would permit little familiarity. The majority of them would never see the bland governess in their fiery-haired mistress. Perhaps Mrs. Clayton might catch a glimpse of the truth, but Cara knew she would never tread on the relationship. Glum would know her no matter what she wore or what she looked like. He had an innate honesty that cut right to the core of everything, and he would recognize her. That pleased Cara, and a smile flitted across her face as she relished the expression on his face as he plumbed her secret.

Restless at Cara's woolgathering, Gentian whickered softly. Touching the velvety neck, she soothed the mare with a gentle stroking motion. A movement halfway down the hill caught Cara's attention, and immediately she tensed, senses alert to danger.

Astride Tyrr, Julian was riding up the hill, heading directly toward her.

Wheeling the mare around, Cara cut back into the woods, seeking the safety of the trees to cover her movements. She did not know if Julian had seen her but could not afford to take the chance of running into him. Once in the woods, Cara pulled Gentian to a halt, forcing down the panic that assailed her. She tried to breathe slowly, concentrating as she organized her thoughts.

Julian was between her and the Hall. She couldn't risk heading back to the stables until she was reasonably sure that he was not close enough to spot her. Possibly he was merely out for a ride, but Cara had a premonition in her bones that he was looking for her. There was no point in running further afield, although the blind panic she had felt when she spied Julian urged her to flight. If he had seen her, he would assume that she was heading away from Weathersfield. The only strategy that she could think of was to wait until he had ridden past and then to bolt for the stables.

With that thought in mind, Cara's eyes quickly surveyed the woods. Because of the abundance of large trees, there was a minimum of undergrowth. Pressured by the fear that at any moment Julian would come bursting through the trees, Cara quickly decided on a rough hiding place. Guiding Gentian toward a small thicket, she sprang to the ground, whispering and coaxing the disapproving animal into the circle of bushes. The mare snorted indignantly when a branch scratched against her coat, the sound loud in the quiet of the forest. Cara regretted wearing the soft gray riding habit. The ugly brown one would have blended well to camouflage her presence. She hoped the lighter material would not act as a beacon, catching Julian's eye. The success of her plan was based on the theory that he would be moving quickly and not spend time inspecting every clump of trees and bushes.

It was only a matter of moments before the crackling of breaking twigs heralded Julian's approach.

Despite the profusion of leaves on the trees, Tyrr and his rider stood out starkly against the dominant yellows and greens of the woods. Cara, trembling in her hiding place, drew in her breath at the sheer magnificence of her husband. Eyes warm with love, she traced the stark features of his face, lingering at the full lips of his sensual mouth. In heightened awareness she wondered what it would be like to be made love to by this man, whose whole body pulsed with a dangerous masculinity. Her heart fluttered in imagined rapture, and she leaned toward him, caught up in the tumult of her own passions.

Julian reined in on the edge of the forest, glancing first uphill and then down. As his eyes brushed her hiding place,

Cara closed her own eyes, afraid they would act as a magnet, drawing his piercing eyes to her. Laying her head against Gentian's neck, she held firmly to the mare's nose with one hand while she gentled the animal with slow, steady caresses. Tyrr threw back his head, snorting and blowing. Then, as though Julian had come to a decision, he nudged the horse into an easy lope, moving uphill.

Cara breathed a shuddering sigh of relief as the horse and rider disappeared through the trees. Despite her hammering pulses, she waited patiently until the woods were once again quiet before she felt it was safe to move.

Whispering and coaxing, Cara backed Gentian out of the thicket. With shaking hands she dragged the horse over to a fallen log. Pulling herself into the saddle, she once again cautiously made her way to the edge of the field. Elation filled her as she viewed the vista, empty of a black stallion and rider. She blew out her cheeks in a rush of relief. The muscles in her thighs still jumped in tension, and she made a concerted effort not to transmit her turmoil to the horse. She steadied her breathing as she picked twigs and leaves out of her disordered hair. Finally, she tossed her head at the empty landscape and clucked gleefully to Gentian as she directed the mare back to the stables.

Cara was about midfield when she heard the thunder of hooves and saw Julian break through the cover of trees.

Without thought she sawed on Gentian's reins, swerving to the right, flying toward a thin band of trees. Lying low across the mare's neck, she heard the pounding of hooves coming closer. In full panic now, she let her horse have its head, mindlessly racing away from Julian.

Julian frankly admitted to himself that he had become slightly obsessed by the mystery girl he had seen in the woods. Every morning he had ridden over as much of the woods as possible without catching so much as a glimpse of the girl with the flaming hair and lithe body.

There was something about the girl that intrigued him, some familiarity of movement that he wanted to observe at closer quarters. He acknowledged the fact that her supple body and beautiful red-gold hair had stirred his senses, but he also was aware that he was filled with rage at how easily she had snubbed him. And she definitely had snubbed him! When he had originally seen her, he had purposely slowed Tyrr's gait, so that he would arrive at her side composed for an introduction, rather than puffing and wheezing from the exertion of his ride. But the contrary girl had used the opportunity to leap upon that misbegotten horse of hers and fly over the wall to sanctuary. Julian was too used to female adulation not be affronted by this blatant cut.

Assuming the girl either lived in the vicinity or was visiting someone close at hand, Julian had begun a round of social calls to the other landowners in the neighborhood. Even at a distance Julian was able to recognize the class and dignity of the rider and the superior bloodstock of the horse. After a frustrating inspection of the daughters, wives, and visiting relatives of his neighbors, he was furious that he still had not discovered the identity of the girl.

The matchmaking mamas in the households where he called were in high alt that he had condescended to visit. He had sat in countless drawing rooms, balancing interminable cups of lukewarm tea while a host of simpering maidens were paraded before his eyes. Although his neighbors were aware of his marital status, it seemed that since there was no bride in evidence, he was still considered semieligible. He had never been comfortable doing the pretty, and this excess of socializing reminded him of why he had accepted complacently, if not eagerly, his father's arrangement of a suitable marriage. The greedy, calculating looks of the mothers was a ludicrous contrast to the blushing innocence of the daughters they were delighted to thrust in his path.

Julian had no idea why it was so necessary to find the

young horsewoman. For some unknown reason it was important. He rationalized that he only wanted to see if her face matched the promise of the rest of her body and to teach the immature chit proper manners. In his more sanguine moments Julian found it wonderful that only since his marriage had two fascinating women entered his life. First, the enigmatic Miss Farraday, and now the unknown girl in the woods.

After all the households were visited and there was still no hint of the horsewoman, he had fallen back on laying a trap for her. He had avoided riding at dawn in hopes that she would return to a pattern that had struck him as a familiar routine. And finally it had paid off.

When Julian spotted the girl on the edge of the woods, he swore loudly, realizing that he was too far down the hill to catch her. Spurring angrily to the top, he plunged into the first line of trees, then reined in in frustration. She was nowhere in sight. He slapped his leather quirt against his boot and scowled blackly at the surrounding trees. It was almost magical how the girl had disappeared so quickly. Knowing that the woods spread out for miles, Julian could only make a guess in which direction she had gone.

"Unless"—he smiled cunningly—"like a fox, she's gone to ground."

The more he thought of the idea the more reasonable it sounded. The woods were curiously silent, and according to his reckoning, she would not have had enough time to outdistance him totally. Somewhere she was lying low, waiting until he gave up the hunt. Tyrr stamped and snorted, throwing his black mane in the air. The stallion sensed the nearness of the mare and, like his master, longed to give chase. Julian nudged the eager horse forward, setting an easy pace toward the top of the hill. He purposely rode without hesitation to give the impression that he had made up his mind. But instead of going deeper into the woods, he guided the horse toward the trees that edged the meadow. Once there, he pulled Tyrr to a halt and leaped to the ground, holding the stallion steady.

Julian reasoned that he had seen the girl on the edge of the meadow, waiting to cross it. If he was right that she was in cover to escape him, she should return to the meadow once she was convinced he was riding away. With the patience of a hunter, Julian waited to spring the trap.

As the first sounds of movement came to his ears, he tensed, reaching up to stroke the stallion whose ears were pricked forward in anticipation. He could see nothing through the heavily leaved trees. Julian waited, his breath streaming steadily through flared nostrils and his eyebrows lowered over cold, steely eyes. When he saw the girl sitting her horse at the edge of the woods, he heaved a sigh of satisfaction mixed with admiration.

She certainly was a beauty, Julian admitted grimly. Well worth the trouble he had gone to. Though at a distance her features were indistinct, her sun-bronzed hair floated around her in a burnished cloud. Silhouetted against the foliage, her figure stood out in sharp relief. Her eyes were narrowed as she searched the meadow, so he could not identify their color, but he suspected they were flashing with triumph that she had outwitted him. She sat the gray expertly, at home with the discomfort of a sidesaddle. He watched with burning eyes as she leaned down, patting the neck of the dainty horse. Then with a light, tinkling laugh that floated across to Julian's straining ears, the lovely vision tossed her hair over her shoulders and trotted jauntily out into the field.

Tyrr caught the scent of the mare and threw his head back soundlessly against Julian's restraining hand.

"Steady, boy. They'll not get away this time." There was a flash of white teeth against sun-browned skin as Julian's predatory gaze followed the figure of the girl. "We'll let her relax and then we'll introduce ourselves." He chuckled mirthlessly.

Julian's relentless eyes stalked the horse and rider until they approached the middle of the field. Then, in a single fluid movement, he released the stallion and threw himself into the saddle. Tyrr, quivering with anticipation, needed little encouragement to tear after the graceful mare. Julian's chest expanded with the joy and excitement of the chase as they hurtled after the girl.

In blind panic Cara raced across the meadow, heading for the cover of trees at the far side. As they tore through the brush at the edge, she lay against Gentian's neck to avoid the branches that slashed at her face. She realized the futility of her flight as the woods immediately narrowed and fell away to reveal another open field. From the corner of her eye she saw Tyrr's head come alongside her own horse. She groaned as Julian's hand shot out, closing on Gentian's bridle, pulling the mare to a stop. As the two horses slowed, Cara disengaged her knee from the sidesaddle and leapt from the saddle, hitting the ground at a run.

It was a stunned moment before Julian realized the girl was still set on escape.

Cara ran as though pursued by the Devil. She prayed she wouldn't stumble over the uneven ground as she dashed for the safety of the trees. Mindlessly she dodged branches as well as she could, paying little heed to them as they tore at her hair and clothes. Her lungs were near bursting when Julian's arm snaked out, swinging her feet off the ground as he hauled her back against his chest. Exhausted, the will to escape went out of Cara and she collapsed against him, sending them both to the grass in a heap.

In the sudden quiet of the forest, the only sound to be heard was the rasp of labored breathing as the two fought to compose themselves.

Julian's burning eyes flicked across the crumpled figure beside him, her chest heaving as she gulped air into her lungs. Her head was bent, hair billowing around her in flaming disarray. Leaves and small twigs were caught in the silken strands, and without hesitation, Julian reached out to pluck them from her hair. He was filled with exhileration at his triumph, his senses quivering with a heightened awareness. As his fingers touched the burnished tresses, they dug in, as with his other hand he grasped the girl's body in a hard embrace.

The girl gasped, and he felt the whisper of air on his cheek before he lowered his mouth to her parted lips.

Petal-soft skin met his, and he savored the taste of her mouth even as she writhed in his arms. He could feel the tumultuous beat of her heart against his own chest as the tentative kiss grew more demanding. Julian felt a completeness with this unknown girl in his arms. She had haunted and consumed his thoughts, and now he had found her. Yet, with this kiss he had the feeling of discovering a treasure that went far deeper than the mere triumph of the chase. His hand reached up to smooth back the veil of hair that hid her features from his searching eyes.

Blue-green eyes, flashing fire, assailed him as he gasped in recognition.

"Miss Farraday!"

Cara was too stunned by the course of events even to attempt to speak. Her mind and body reeled from the effects of Julian's kiss. Her cheeks burned and her lips tingled. Fighting for time, she sat up, brushing futilely at the stains on her skirts. Knowing herself for a coward, she carefully kept her head bent, thus avoiding the steady brown eyes she knew to be boring into her.

"Have you anything to say, Miss Farraday?" Julian's voice grated out the question as he bolted to his feet and stood towering over the tiny figure.

Cara glanced up in trepidation, wincing at the black scowl on Julian's face and then in a rush spoke the first thought to come into her head.

"Just once I would like you to see me clean," she whispered wistfully.

Julian's face turned red with anger. In weary detachment, Cara watched the veins in his temple throbbing with suppressed emotion. For a moment she wondered if in his anger he might strike her, but was just too exhausted to care. She witnessed the complex of emotions that rippled through Julian's body as he stared down at her own expressionless face. She held her breath as he threw back his head and a great explosion of air burst from his mouth in rolling bellows of laughter. He cast himself down beside the nonplussed girl, still laughing until tears stood in the corners of his eyes.

Positive that the man had become unhinged, Cara edged away, sending Julian into another fit of laughter at the anxious expression on her face. She waited, poised on the edge of flight, as he fought to control his amusement. Finally, his gasps and wheezes quieted, and he stared at her through still watering eyes.

"Miss Farraday, you are a constant amazement to me."

Julian's eyes appraised the girl as though seeing her for the first time. He smiled in approval at what he was now discovering. He should have seen before that she was beautiful, even behind the dowdy dresses and the bound hair. Her skin was flawless, cheeks speckled with freckles and now flushed with exercise and embarrassment. Her blue-green eyes, direct and honest, were wide set and vividly alive. Her mouth was generous and soft, moist as the morning dew.

Feeling Julian's eyes on her mouth, Cara's lips tingled and her heartbeat quickened in remembrance of his kiss. In fear at the sensual look in his eyes, she struggled to her feet. He was there before her, and his arms whipped around her, pinning her helplessly against his chest.

"Please. No," Cara begged hoarsely.

"Before, I kissed a stranger. Now, I at least know who you are."

His mouth came down, covering her trembling lips, and

153

Cara's knees buckled as fire tore through her body. Once more she struggled, pushing futilely at his chest. She had a wild, floating sensation as the blood sang in her veins. She had been frightened by his first kiss, but now she was overwhelmed at the passion his touch aroused. Of their own volition, her hands crept up around his neck, her fingers burning with a desire to feel the texture of his hair. Her body strained against his as her mind whirled in ecstasy.

Although Julian would have no way of knowing, she was desperately in love with him. And loving him, she was totally vulnerable to him, wanting his kisses and caresses, filled with an almost painful need for his closeness. Julian's senses were inflamed as he felt the acquiescence of the girl to his lovemaking. His tongue probed the wetness of her mouth, and he shifted his embrace to cup the soft breast pressed against his chest.

The contact of his hand broke through Cara's swirling emotions, jolting her back to sanity. Frantic to break free, she tore out of his grasp, staggering when he released her. Her hands pressed protectively against her chest as tears of shame started in her eyes. She felt totally humiliated by how easily he had broken through her emotional defenses.

A single tear dropped to her flushed cheek, catching the light and sparkling like a jewel.

Julian flushed with remorse, observing the genuine distress of the girl. He watched the tear slither down her cheek and reached out a finger to touch the wetness. In wonder he felt his heart constrict. The girl was tense, with the alert wariness of a frightened doe. She was prepared to flee at his slightest movement. Julian's hand dropped to his side, and he smiled gently at the trembling girl.

"I apologize, Miss Farraday," he said softly. "If I promise to behave myself, will you stay?"

Cara's eyes searched Julian's, reaching beyond the warm brown eyes to the mind and heart of the man. As though satisfied, she nodded her head, still unable to speak. Julian scanned the area, then indicated a fallen log a short distance away. Without words they walked to it and sat down. He leaned forward, waiting in silence, but still the girl refused to speak or even to meet his glance. Unable to restrain his impatience, he cleared his throat loudly.

"Well, Miss Farraday?" he questioned. Then, at her continued silence, he barked, "Confound it, girl. I can't keep calling you that. I assume you do have a first name."

"Cara" came the whispered reply.

"Cara, then," he snapped. In exasperation he rapped out, "Do you suppose you could look at me while I talk? You owe me at least that courtesy."

He caught his breath as blue-green eyes impaled him with their glittering brightness. Time was suspended as they locked glances. He felt his life telescoped into a moment in time and hesitated to break the contact for fear of losing something very precious. Then, as his vision cleared to take in more of the girl's face, he saw a shift behind her eyes and recognized a look of speculation, and he narrowed his own gaze preparing for trouble.

Now that Cara was out of immediate physical danger, she was able to compose herself. Her mind whirled crazily from one scheme to another. She realized that her discovery by Julian was a consummate disaster and grappled with various ideas on how she could extricate herself from the present dilemma. In despair she fought for time, hoping that she could dodge Julian's questions sufficiently for the moment. Her only real hope was to escape Weathersfield.

"Now, Cara," Julian began sternly, "Have you any explanation for your behavior?"

"I ran away because I didn't think you'd let me ride your cattle. And I do so love riding," she finished ingenuously.

"You know full well that's not what I'm talking about!" Julian burst out in genuine anger. He thrust himself to his

155

feet and paced before her in fury. He clenched and un-clenched his large hands in an excess of frustration. "Your entire act as governess has been a shameless charade!"

"It has not!" Cara defended herself. With dignity she rose to her feet, facing the furious man with an anger of her own. "I have been a perfect governess. Well, almost perfect," she faltered.

"But you've lied throughout," he stormed. "Your dowdy clothes, mousy behavior, and—oh, ho—your pitiful show of unhorsemanship," he accused. "What a bravura performance. You have missed your calling, my dear. You should definitely be on the stage."

"You, sir, hired me to be a governess to your wards. You did not hire me to strut around in fancy dresses and ride to the hounds."

In high dudgeon Cara whirled and stalked off toward the meadow. Julian stood thunderstruck. The haughty wench fully intended to bluster her way out of this. Shaking his head in disbelief, he strode after her, catching hold of her arm as she stepped out into the field.

"Miss Farraday!" he bellowed. "I want a full explanation of this entire affair!"

"You are hurting my arm, sir," Cara said coldly, staring down in disdain to where his gloved hand dug into the material of her sleeve.

Infuriated beyond control, Julian flung her arm away, striding after her as she continued to walk calmly toward the horses, who were peacefully grazing. Glancing up through her lashes, Cara suspected that Julian was close to apoplexy. His breathing was ragged, and his jaw was set dangerously. Stopping abruptly, she turned to face him.

"Lord Wilton, I was a woman alone in England," Cara began, trying to stick as closely as she could to the truth without giving away too much. "I wanted the position as governess, but for my own protection I chose to dress in

156

clothes that would make me acceptable to being hired. I wanted to be inconspicuous.''

"You, my dear, could never be inconspicuous," Julian snapped sarcastically.

"But I think you will agree that I did do the job I was hired to do," continued Cara, as though she had not been interrupted. "If it's any consolation, I have already made plans to leave your employ."

"No, Miss Farraday, you will not be leaving," replied Julian ominously. "At least not until I get to the bottom of this business."

Trying to hide how much his words had shaken her, Cara permitted him to give her a leg up. Then, with back straight and head held high, she rode beside Julian down the hill toward the Hall.

Chapter Eleven

Glum came running as the two horses trotted into the stable yard. He shrugged in futility as he met Julian's accusing stare. Noting the disheveled girl, he hurried to help her dismount. Cara patted his arm comfortingly and gave him the faintest glimmer of an apologetic smile.

"Miss Farraday," Julian ground out. "If you please, after you have changed, I will see you in my office." Then, leaning close to her ear, he snarled, "And don't attempt to do anything foolish." Turning toward Glum, whose face was bleak with resignation, he barked, "Miss Farraday is not to ride for the remainder of her stay with us."

Julian stormed off toward the Hall, and Cara's shoulders slumped in defeat. She tried to put on a brave front for the old man who looked so woebegone, but sheer exhaustion left her close to tears.

"Don't worry, Glum," she said in a ragged voice. "I'll tell him it was all my fault. I promise you won't lose your job." Cara only hoped that would be true.

"Never mind, miss. His Lordship be a hard man, but he's a fair one. Perhaps it'll all blow over," he added wistfully.

"Perhaps," Cara agreed weakly.

Her feet dragged as she made her way to her room. Wearily she stared around the room that had become so familiar to her. Tears pricked her lids, but she shook her head, refusing to give up all hope. Crossing the room, she faltered as she spied a letter on her desk. Picking it up, she knew without opening it that it was a note from her grandmother. She smiled wanly, wondering which chambermaid had been bribed to bring the letter to her room. No doubt the girl thought it was some romantic billet-doux. Shrugging in defeat, she tossed the letter on her quilt.

"If only the letter had come yesterday," Cara moaned.

She winced as she imagined what her grandmother would say about her present predicament. Her mind whirled, and in confusion she thought of what a muddle she had made of everything. Raising a shaking hand to her burning cheek, she tried to remember her original plan and discover when it had first gone wrong.

She should have followed her grandmother's advice and remained anonymous. Then she would have returned to the duchess and, in the proper setting, been presented to Julian as his new bride. With a dazzling hairdo and luxurious clothing, he would have never recognized in the radiant incomparable the timid governess so recently in his employ. In his ignorance there would have been no injury to his pride, Cara reasoned.

But now that Julian had seen her singular hair color and had actually become interested enough in her as a person, the deception would be exposed. Cara quaked at his reaction to this impersonation.

She honestly had never considered how Julian would feel if he discovered her within his household. Now as she thought about it, she suspected that he would be furious. Surely he would have some right to be incensed that she had invaded his household under false pretenses in order to spy on him. In retrospect she wondered how the duchess could have countenanced such an incredible scheme.

Knowing that time was rapidly slipping away, Cara tried to consider her options. She knew she could never bluster her way through this scrape. Squaring her shoulders, she acknowledged the fact that the only possible course of action was a full confession of her deception. She would just have to wait to see what Julian's reaction would be before deciding her next move.

Washing quickly, she changed into a fresh dress. It was a soft lavender-blue muslin with simple, demure lines complemented by a virginal white collar and cuffs. It was the only dress in her meager wardrobe that fit her perfectly while still giving the impression of an insignificant governess. Vigorously brushing her hair, she braided it and then covered it entirely with a matching headdress. In the mirror her image appeared prim and timorous, except for the splotch of vibrant color brushed across her cheeks. Turning away from the glass, she once again picked up the letter, and opened it.

As she had expected, it was from her grandmother, instructing her to explain she had been called to London. The letter further explained that a carriage would be sent in the late afternoon to fetch her. A sad smile flitted across Cara's face as she appreciated the irony of the situation. After this debacle the carriage would not be bringing her back in triumph.

Sighing, she thrust the letter into the pocket of her dress. Straightening her shoulders, she hurried to the main staircase, determined to make as good a show of her confession as possible. The footmen she passed studiously avoided her eyes, telling Cara more surely than words that Julian was in a tearing bad temper. Taking a deep breath, she scratched the door of the study and entered.

Julian sat at the desk frowning down at a paper in his hands. He had washed, and Cara noticed that the black curls still shone with dampness. Her eyes caressed his handsome features, and her heart fluttered as she once again felt the imprint of his lips on her own. In confusion, she averted her eyes, looking down at her feet.

Glancing up, Julian cocked an eyebrow at the transformation of the girl. Seeing her so demurely clothed and with her hair bound, he found it incredible to believe she was the passionate creature of the forest. Eyes lowered and cheeks flushed with maidenly blushes, she was once again the innocuous little governess. It was only when she raised her eyes that he recognized his wood's nymph.

"Before you start berating me, please understand that Glum was not to blame for assisting me in my deception," Cara blurted out before Julian could speak. "He thought he was protecting me from unwanted attention. It was all my fault. Truly it was."

Cara stumbled to a halt as Julian's eyes flared in fury. His hands crumpled the paper he held, but she knew he was wishing it were her neck. She gulped in terror, closing her eyes, half-swooning as he vaulted to his feet. When nothing happened, she dared to peek at him through her lashes. He was braced with both fists on the desk, leaning toward her. The set of his jaw and the tension in his coiled body left little doubt that she was in for a bad time.

"You continue to amaze me, Miss Farraday!" Julian shouted across the desk. "You would think if someone was in the unenviable position you are in, she would at least have enough sense to do everything possible to make amends. She would certainly not enter a room and immediately upbraid her employer."

Cara flushed at the justice of his words. It seemed her impetuous tongue was going to continue to get her into trouble. She raised stricken, teary eyes to Julian's enraged face.

"I'm sorry," she whispered.

"Oh, sit down." Julian's voice was tired, and he ran a hand around behind his neck as he straightened. He stared at her a moment longer, then threw himself back into his chair. His gaze was frosty as she daintily sat on the edge of the leather chair across from his desk.

Although it was only breakfast time for the rest of the household, Cara felt as though an entire day had passed. Anxiously she clutched her hands together in her lap. She felt Julian's eyes boring into her huddled figure, but she refused to meet his gaze. The silence lengthened in the tension-filled room.

"I would dearly love to remain here and beat the truth out of you." Julian's softly spoken words sent a thrill of terror through Cara, and she raised wide eyes to his face. For a moment, staring into the startled depths, he felt his senses whirling in confusion, and he lost his train of thought. Then, nerving himself, he continued. "However I have been summoned to London, and I am leaving immediately."

Cara's breath was expelled in a feathery sigh. She had prayed for a miracle but had not entertained much hope. Perhaps now she could find a way out of her dilemma. Julian watched her through narrowed eyes. Noticing the girl's returning color, he snorted in annoyance.

"I am sure that you will put the time to good use. I expect that by the time I return, you will have concocted quite a suitable story to explain this . . ." Words failed him, and he waved his hand in exasperation.

Cara refused to be baited, staring back at Julian boldly, then lowering her eyes when she sensed the light of battle within his own dark brown ones.

"Wouldn't it just be easier for us both if when you returned, you found I was already gone?" Cara ventured reasonably.

"No!" Julian exploded.

The girl rose from her chair, ready to flee, but he was too quick for her. As she raced for the door, he was before her, so that she skidded to a stop, almost catapulting herself against the hard wall of his chest. Julian grabbed her shoulders, catching his breath as an electric shock coursed through his hands and arms as he touched her.

Seeing the blaze of passion in the brown eyes, Cara tried to twist away, but he drew her toward him until her mouth was only inches away from his own. Julian could feel the girl's heart pounding in her body and watched as her face whitened and her eyes darkened with fear. He seemed to be sinking in the pools of blue-green as he bent his head to touch her lips in a kiss of infinite tenderness. He caught her as her knees buckled, holding her in an embrace that was at once protective and yet intensely passionate.

"Whatever am I going to do with you, Miss Farraday?" he asked in genuine bafflement.

Cara forced her spinning senses into some semblance of order. She leaned back against his arm, breathing through reddened lips that still pulsed with the imprint of his kiss. "Let me go, Lord Wilton." Cara purposely used his title, hoping to remind him of the impropriety of his actions.

"I'm sorry, Miss Farraday, but that is something I find I am extremely loath to do." However, he did release her, leaning casually against the doorframe.

"I was hired as your wards' governess, and you have found me unsuitable," Cara began softly, running her tongue over her suddenly dry lips. "You must let me go."

"It is true that I find you totally unfitted for the role of governess," Julian snapped, his teeth flashing in a wolfish grin. "However, I have discovered other qualities in you that make you eminently suitable for another position."

Cara gasped at his insulting words. Her face burned as she realized that her own actions had left her open to this compromising situation. She might be foolhardy, but she was definitely not to be considered a woman of easy virtue. Affronted, she drew herself up, cloaking herself in dignity.

"You, sir, are a married man. I hope with all my heart I have misunderstood your intentions."

"I think, my dear, you are fully cognizant of my intentions."

His eyes roamed insultingly down her body, as if to

emphasize his comment. Tears started in Cara's eyes, and she bent her head so that he would not see her disillusionment. He reached out a hand to stroke the distressed girl, then pulled it back. He would show no pity to the deceitful chit.

"I do not know how many days I will be gone, but when I return, we will make some kind of arrangement. Despite the fact that you have spent the better part of your time in my employ trying to deceive me, I would like your word that you will not leave here."

Nostrils flaring in anger, Cara glared up at him, refusing to answer. Their locked glances held for what seemed hours but was probably only a minute. Sighing in annoyance, Julian squinted through narrowed eyes at the exasperating girl.

"Be reasonable, Cara. I have forbidden you the use of the stables. Even Glum, whose loyalty I would have staked my life on until you came charging into my singularly uneventful existence, wouldn't dare to defy my orders this time. I suppose you might, as a last resort, walk into the village. Even for an Amazon such as yourself, I wouldn't recommend it." He smiled wryly down at the demurely bent head. "With your limitless ingenuity you might contrive to steal a horse. With you, I have discovered almost anything is possible. I would truly dislike locking you up until my return."

As the girl still remained obdurately silent, Julian's voice took on a coaxing tone. "Promise me you will not steal a horse to make your escape."

Thrusting her hand into her pocket, Cara touched the comforting security of her grandmother's letter. Although in her pride she would have preferred to remain silent, she suspected that Julian would never permit her to leave the room unless she promised him something. She had no intention of being locked up. She hoped that if she appeared to be resigned to her fate, he might not look further into her easy acquiescence. Forcing her voice to a colorless tone, she tentatively raised her expressionless face to Julian.

"I promise I will not steal a horse." Cara's voice trembled, adding credence to her words. She gritted her teeth as Julian, after searching her face, grinned in triumph.

"Thank you, Miss Farraday. I will accept your word. Until my return."

Julian opened the door to let her pass, bowing graciously. It took all of Cara's self-control not to kick him as he stood gracefully balanced on one leg. Her foot literally itched to make contact with his shin, and she had to force herself to hurry past him before she succumbed to the overpowering urge. Unaware of her thoughts, Julian chuckled as she flew up the stairs, running as though pursued by demons.

Regaining her room, Cara closed the door softly, pressing down the desire to slam it shut so that the sound would reverberate through the Hall. She leaned against the wood, her breath coming in gasping little pants. She was trembling with anger and crossed her arms over her chest, holding in the scream of rage that threatened to overwhelm her. How dared he? she fumed. Squeezing her eyes shut, she tried to breathe calmly, forcing her disordered emotions into some sort of reasonable thought. Slowly the heartbeat pounding in her ears began to ebb to a more even rhythm. Pulling herself away from the support of the door, she crossed the floor to the window seat, flinging herself down on the cushions.

Leaning her forehead against the cool glass, she stared blindly over the gardens toward the lake. Bleakly she viewed her future, which to her agonized mind held less hope than when she had started her masquerade as governess.

Cara loved Julian wildly, passionately, and without reservation. She was fully aware of his faults, yet he had begun to represent for her the ideal husband. She had thought several times that he had reciprocated her own feelings of affinity. In her more hopeful moments she had even imagined that one day he might truly love her.

The scene in the library came back to her in all its stark reality, and she flinched inwardly at her own innocence.

She herself had planned to enter into the arranged marriage with a spirit of resolution that, working together, they might have a successful union. She had been willing to try, at least. But it was perfectly apparent to her that Julian had no such idea; he did not even plan to keep his marriage vows. He had all but declared that he intended to make her his mistress, willing or not. Even when she had charged him with his married state, he had sneered at her naïveté. And on the very eve of his bride's arrival!

Worst for Cara was the humiliation she felt at what a fool she had been to think he had reciprocated her feelings. He had seen her only as an object to assuage his raging lust. While she had opened her heart to him, he had only eyed her physical attributes, content to toy with her emotions. At least, once he realized who she really was, she would have the satisfaction of telling him exactly what she thought of his behavior.

What would Julian do then? Cara wondered apprehensively.

Tremulously Cara wondered if he might not repudiate the marriage. Even the thought of it filled her with an agonizing feeling of loss. If he divorced her, she might be able to live with the shame of it, but never to see Julian again was an insupportable thought. Of course, his other alternative was to accept the marriage but make it merely a sham relationship. In his anger and pride he might leave her alone in the country and continue his life in London as he had done in his bachelor days. Lady Valencia Greeley's catlike face floated across Cara's consciousness. Sobbing, Cara pressed the back of her hand to her mouth as she thought of the humiliation of being forced to accept Julian's return to his mistress.

"Enough!" Cara exclaimed aloud. She was no weak-kneed maiden. No matter the outcome of this nasty coil, she would accept it with dignity. She bathed her face, mentally fortifying the white-faced girl in the mirror. Through the door to the schoolroom, she could hear the happy chatter of the children. Straightening her shoulders, she reminded herself that she still had a job to do until her grandmother's carriage arrived to take her back to London.

Cara never knew how she got through the remainder of the day. She had been subdued but had otherwise conducted herself fairly normally. Later she was never able to remember much about her last day at the Hall.

As the hands of the clock crept steadily toward the time of her departure, Cara waited impatiently for the arrival of Richard and Belin. Her portmanteau was packed, and there were only the children to deal with. She had inveigled Mrs. Clayton into providing a lavish snack, earlier in the evening than usual. Praying that everything might, by some miracle, work out, she pasted a smile on her face as she heard the clatter of feet outside the schoolroom.

"Oh, Richard. Look at all the food," Belin chirped happily, her fingers reaching out to hover over the cream-filled buns, which were her favorite. "What a wonderful surprise, Miss Farraday."

"It looks like a grand party. Is Uncle Julian coming?" Richard's face lit up with anticipation.

"No, Richard," Cara said quickly. Then after the chorus of groans had subsided, "Your uncle had to make an urgent trip to London. He should be back in a few days."

"Well, it's lovely, anyway," Belin pronounced, sighing with pleasure as she bit into one of the buns.

"Why the party, Miss Farraday?" Richard asked in a surprisingly adult voice.

Being older, Richard was less easily pacified by the sight

of cream buns than Belin. He stared at her intently from eyes that had seen more tragedies than most children of his age. Perhaps, because of his own experiences he was more sensitive to upheavals. Eyeing Belin joyfully attacking another pastry, Richard gave Cara a speaking glance, then leaned over to pour out the hot chocolate with a hand that shook only slightly.

"It's really not all that bad, Richard," Cara whispered softly. Reaching out, she ruffled his hair; then, smiling, she brushed an errant curl away from his forehead. "Come and sit down."

Momentarily taking her eyes off the pastry-filled silver platter, Belin sensed an almost tangible tension in the air and stopped eating. Her glance swung uneasily from her brother to her governess and then back again to Richard.

"I thought it would be fun to have a little party ourselves," Cara began haltingly. Then seeing the wariness in the eyes of the children, she hurried ahead. "I have to go up to London, also. I'm not sure just how long it will take, but I have to attend to some business."

"But who will take care of us?" Belin lisped.

Tears started in Belin's eyes as she wailed out the question. Cara opened up her arms, and the child climbed into the temporary safety of her governess's lap. Leaning against Cara's shoulder, Belin sniffled in her distress. Looking over the jumble of black curls to the boy beyond, Cara was surprised to see angry color rise to Richard's face.

"Did Uncle Julian send you down?" the boy asked belligerently.

"Oh, no, Richard," Cara cried in distress.

"Was it because of the row this morning?" He ignored Cara's protest and hurried on. "I heard a lot of yelling this morning, and Mrs. Clayton said that you were in the library with Uncle Julian. When he's mad and tearing a strip off one, his voice shakes the pictures in the long gallery."

The boy shook his head in sympathy. "Pennyfeather says Uncle Julian's more wind than damage."

Cara wasn't surprised that Richard was aware of the morning's contretemps. It was not as though Julian had made any attempt to conceal his anger. And, of course, the servants always knew everything that went on in the Hall. Since the children had the run of the kitchen, they were privy to much of the gossip that was passed back and forth over a cup of tea.

"I suppose I'd better explain." Cara sighed in resignation. She had hoped the children would accept the fact that she would be gone for several days and not look too closely at her story. She hesitated, unsure of how to proceed. "It is true that your Uncle Julian was angry with me. He found me out riding this morning, and I had not asked his permission to use one of the horses. You know how particular he is about his cattle."

"But why were you riding, Miss Farraday?" Richard's forehead was wrinkled in bafflement, remembering the last time that he had seen Cara on a horse.

"I was practicing," Cara improvised glibly.

"Oh, I see." The story was obviously acceptable to the boy. Then, remembering again her last ride, Richard broke into a mischievous grin. "I can see Uncle Julian now. He probably thought you were abusing his precious horse. What a facer that must have been."

"Now, as to your question, young lady. Mrs. Clayton has agreed to look after you." As a frown began to form on the child's face, Cara offered quickly. "She has a lovely new sampler she thought you might like to try. And I hoped you would like to help Cook in the kitchen. She might even teach you how to make those sugar buns you like."

Thus reminded of the remaining food, Belin scrambled down and once more launched herself at the plate of goodies. Richard looked warily at Cara, waiting for word of his fate.

"I thought you might like to help Glum in the stables."
She smiled at the lightened look in Richard's eyes. "One
day you will be setting up your own stables, and there's a
lot you will have to know. You'll work with him until your
uncle returns."

Richard didn't comment immediately. He searched her
face to see if there was something else she wanted to say.
Then he shrugged as if to say that even though he was not
totally satisfied, he would do what she had instructed.

Cara's eyes swam at the perception of the boy. Leaning
forward, she blinked her eyes to clear her vision before she
was able to pour more hot chocolate. The children chattered away, but she had little heart to join in as she usually
did. Too soon, it was time for Cara to leave. Hugging
Belin, she reminded her to be good for Mrs. Clayton and
to remember her manners. Promising she would buy her a
present in London, she held the squirming child to her
heart for one last hard squeeze.

Richard stood very straight in the doorway. He brushed
the toe of his boot on the back of his trouser leg. Then,
looking directly up at Cara, he sighed.

"You will be coming back again, Miss Farraday?" he
asked with a suddenly shaking voice. "Please?"

Cara knelt down in front of the boy, her dress spreading
out prettily around her. Rather like flower petals, he
thought. In fact, Miss Farraday really was like a flower,
with her shining face so close to his and the scent of her
perfume filling his nose. He hadn't realized how pretty she
was until just this minute. She certainly was a smasher,
though.

"I know you're worried," began Cara. "But I'm hoping
that I will be back very soon. There's something I have to
settle first. But I promise you, Richard, that I will come
back and explain if, for any reason, I have to go away
permanently. Will that be acceptable?"

"Yes, I guess so." For one awkward minute the child's

chin trembled, but he quickly got his expression under control. "But if it's all right, I'd really rather you'd come to stay here forever."

"Thank you, Richard."

Cara put her arms around the boy, who at first stiffened and then yielded, throwing his own arms around her. They hugged tightly, then she gave him a little push down the hall toward his room.

Richard reflected that it hadn't been so bad being hugged by Miss Farraday, even if he was a little old for that baby stuff. He bet if Uncle Julian hugged her once, he wouldn't be half so mad about the horses. But then, grown-ups were funny. Uncle Julian might not like hugging very much.

For her part, Cara was busy clearing up after the children. She dried her eyes and tried not to think about Belin and Richard. She had no way of knowing whether Julian, in his anger, would permit her to see the children again. If he wanted a divorce, she knew in her heart she would not fight him. She would prefer the disgrace of rejection and the scandal it engendered than to have a husband who did not love her. However, no matter what was decided about her own future, she would force Julian to let her see the children and explain if she would be going away permanently. They had already suffered enough losses in their young lives. They were fond of her, and they trusted her, so that she could never go away without first seeing them one last time. She loved the children dearly, and no matter what it cost her pride, she would insist that Julian allow her that.

Summoned at the arrival of the coach, Cara clutched her portmanteau and walked stiffly on leaden feet down the main staircase. Mrs. Clayton waited for her, her plump face creased with an anxious frown. Cara had only told her that she would send word when, and if, she would return. Like the other servants, the housekeeper was well aware of the argument with Julian. Eyes bright with unshed tears, the two women hugged with genuine affection.

Ceremoniously handed into the luxurious coach, Cara settled herself into the plush cushions. Wearily she leaned her head against the soft upholstery, forcing herself not to look back as Weathersfield was swallowed up in the early evening gloom. Vowing she would use the time to order her muddled thoughts and feelings, the exhausted girl tumbled quickly into a restless slumber as the horses bore her unconscious figure to London and her fate.

Chapter Twelve

"Offhand, my child, I'd say you've made a fine muddle of things." Cara's grandmother, Liela, spoke dryly to the misty-eyed girl who slumped in the chair across from her. She had listened intently as the story unfolded, but even more carefully, she had watched the play of emotion on Cara's face and the unspoken words behind her faltering explanations.

"I'm terribly sorry, Grandmother. Really I am." Cara spoke with sincerity as she woefully eyed the older woman. "I really did try to stay in the background. It all just seemed to happen without my having any control. Please don't be angry, Gran."

"I'm not angry, Cara."

At her grandmother's warm words, Cara glanced up in surprise. It was true. The duchess didn't look angry. In general, she looked pleased, and there was almost a smug, satisfied gleam in her eyes. Although puzzled by the older woman's manner, the girl hurried on.

"At least, there isn't any open scandal. At least, not yet. Luckily Julian was called away," Cara explained. Then, as Liela continued to smile, Cara's eyes opened wide in wonder. "The paper he was reading. It was a letter. And, if my guess is correct, you sent it."

"The letter I think you are referring to, Cara, was one

I sent to Lord Wilton requesting his presence most urgently. After all, with Julian at Weathersfield, it would have been difficult to send a carriage to collect you without his suspecting something was rather havey-cavey. Of course, when I penned the note, I had no idea you were in such a tight fix.''

"You mean, Julian is here?" Cara gasped, leaping to her feet.

"No. No. Softly, child. Remember, it's late and I am still an old woman." The duchess chuckled throatily at the snort of disbelief from her cheeky granddaughter. "When Lord Wilton arrived, he was instructed to return in the morning. I imagine he's safely ensconced in one of his clubs, working off his frustration by drinking with his cronies. Men have a difficult time dealing with the crotchets of old ladies.''

"But what will I say to him? What will I do?"

The duchess watched in amusement as Cara paced restlessly across the carpet. It reminded her sharply of a similar scene just a month ago. Then, the girl had been decrying the existence of her marriage; now, she was terrified that this same marriage might be terminated.

All in all, the older woman was well pleased. It appeared that the child must have some sort of feeling for Julian. Although Cara had continually spoken of her fondness for the children, the duchess could see the pain that crossed the girl's face when her husband's name was mentioned. There were some obvious gaps in Cara's story during which, Liela suspected, Julian had acted less than gentlemanly. Apparently he had drawn the line at actually compromising her granddaughter.

"Are you in love with Wilton?''

Cara's head snapped up and she glared defiantly. For a moment the duchess expected she would answer in the negative. Then the girl sighed wearily, settling herself on the soft carpeting in front of her grandmother.

"I'm afraid so, Gran," she whispered softly. "I love him with all my heart."

Smiling down at Cara's radiant face, the duchess remembered her own impetuous romance. Her gnarled fingers smoothed the reddish curls away from the girl's soft white forehead. One beringed hand traced down the soft cheek and cupped the firm chin. "Then, my child, you'll just have to wait and see what we can do."

"But he'll be so angry." Cara winced, imagining Julian's fury.

"Perhaps. Men are rarely amused by a woman's machinations. Even though our manipulations are generally for their own good," she finished spiritedly. "At any rate, there's no point in getting into a pother until we hear from Julian. No need to rush your fences."

The duchess yawned, covering her mouth delicately with her blue-veined hands. Then she patted the girl once more.

"It's already past midnight, Cara. Tomorrow will be another day. Time then to resolve all these problems." Cara helped the old woman to her feet. "It will be pleasant dealing with your troubles in the daytime, my dear. Every time you appear, I am kept much too late from my bed," she reproved; then her expression softened. "I have the feeling that no matter what tomorrow brings, I will be pleased to have you here in England."

"Good night, Gran," Cara said, kissing the wrinkled cheek gently. "I'm glad to be here with you, too. No matter what."

But Cara's brave words disappeared quickly as she lay sleepless in her bed. Over and over she remembered Julian's anger and his insulting suggestions. No matter what happened, she feared she would be unhappy with the outcome. The bright morning brought little relief to Cara's mind. She breakfasted with her grandmother but could barely swallow any of her food. The duchess refused to discuss anything until after she had seen and talked to Julian. Until then, Cara must be content to wait.

When he was announced, Cara was directed to the garden until the duchess sent someone for her. The last thing she saw was the regal figure of her grandmother seated in a thronelike chair in the salon. The older woman was dressed in pearl-encrusted midnight-blue silk. White lace ruffles at neck and wrists were spattered with brilliants, and in her ring-covered hands she gripped a malacca walking stick with an enormous ruby embedded in the top. Cara almost pitied Julian in his interview with the intimidating duchess.

Cara strolled amid the flowerbeds, hoping that the gentle beauty of her surroundings would ease the tension of the morning. Birds flitted from tree to tree, and as she rounded a bend in the walk, two rabbits streaked ahead of her, disappearing under a hedge. When she reached the gazebo, she sank dispiritedly onto the cushioned seat.

For a while she tried to read the book of poetry she had brought with her but found that although her eyes skimmed the words on the page, her brain refused to register their meaning. Finally, she leaned her head wearily against one of the pillars and closed her eyes.

"Cara!"

The angry shout brought Cara instantly awake, and she shook her head to clear the cobwebs that had coated her brain. Striding furiously along the path was Julian. The flash of fury on his face banished her hopes, and she turned to flee.

Julian bounded up the steps, grasping Cara's wrist before she could get away. Whirling her around, he speared the girl with the intensity of his gaze. He caught his breath as he stared down at her. The baggy-dressed governess was gone, and in her place was an exquisite creature he barely recognized.

Cara wore a celestial-blue gauze frock, tied beneath her

breasts with varicolored ribbons. The simple lines and clinging material emphasized the rounded curves of her body. Her hair, which Julian had seen only once, floated around her face and hung down her back in a glorious halo of burnished curls. Flushed with discomfort, her face was the creamy rose of a healthy complexion. For a moment he stared down at the quaking figure with admiration, but when his eyes touched her blue-green ones, his anger was rekindled.

"You gave me your word you wouldn't leave Weathersfield!" he barked accusingly. "I find it unpardonable that you should break it."

"I didn't!" Cara shouted back at him, insulted that he should mistrust her so. "You made me promise that I would not steal a horse. And I didn't," she finished triumphantly.

"You are the most infuriatingly annoying young woman it has ever been my misfortune to meet!"

"And you, sir, are the most arrogant, insensitive person that I have ever known!"

Cara flung away from Julian, moving back against the wooden railing of the gazebo. Her chest rose and fell rapidly with the rush of emotion racing through her veins at his presence. Peeking at Julian through the lacy network of her eyelashes, she acknowledged that his face was slightly haggard, but despite that, he was so handsome that Cara felt her heart swell with pride.

"Why aren't you still at Weathersfield? How did you get here?" Julian's questions shot out rapidly, permitting no reply from the startled girl. "And what the devil are you doing in the duchess's gardens?"

"You seem to have forgotten, Lord Wilton, that I came to your employ through the helpful services of the duchess. She sent for me not long after you left Weathersfield."

"I had forgotten; so much has happened since that time." Julian ran his hand through his hair in agitation. He seemed distracted, for all his anger. His face was baffled as well as furious. In frustration he jerked her arm roughly, pulling her toward a bench along the side of the tiny structure.

"Sit down, Cara." Julian spoke harshly, but despite the fierceness of voice, his hands were gentle as he pushed her onto the bench. "I must talk with you. It may be the last chance we'll ever have."

Cara's heart jolted with the pain of his words. The interview with her grandmother must have gone very badly indeed. She had hoped, at least, for some kind of hearing, but by his words it was evident that Julian had made up his mind to reject her. In agony she stared at her hands, praying for the strength to endure the discussion with some dignity. But it was so difficult, she thought, biting her trembling lip. She loved Julian so much that the thought of never seeing him again was almost more than she could bear, either mentally or physically.

"I asked the duchess to begin annulment proceedings."

Julian flung himself away from Cara, as though her very presence was repugnant to him. As he paced back and forth in front of her, Cara's mind refused to take in any of his other words. Her heart actually felt as though it were breaking at his harsh statement. She had expected him to be angry, but she had always held out some hope that he would show some understanding.

In a small voice she asked, "Is there no hope for us?"

"No!" The bald syllable tore across Cara's heart, and for a moment blackness engulfed her. Fighting against the swoon, she tried to sit straighter, but her whole body trembled at his next words.

"The duchess has suggested that you be sent back to America on one of the ships belonging to her family."

"Oh, no," Cara wailed. At least she had hoped to be able to stay in England. Somehow she might even see Julian, although his offended behavior gave her little encouragement that their future meetings would be anything but coldly formal.

"You will leave as soon as arrangements can be made," Julian rasped out.

Keeping her head bent, Cara was able to stem the tears that threatened to overflow. Although inwardly shattered, she attempted to salvage a little of her pride.

"And the children?" she whispered.

"I know the children love you. It will be horrible for them, but they're young and will get over it."

Cara was silent, aghast at the disaster she had created with her scheming. To lose Julian was to lose her life, and now even the children would be gone.

Fidgeting in the silence, Julian finally burst out, "You can see that there is no other way. We cannot be together in the same household."

Cara flinched at his cutting words and glanced up at the face of the man who was her whole world. Julian's features were distorted with anger, and his hands flexed as though he wanted to strangle her.

"Do you hate me so much, then?"

Cara gasped at her own temerity. Then she recoiled as Julian lunged toward her. His hands bit into her shoulders as he hauled her to her feet. In his agitation he shook her until Cara thought her neck might break.

"Hate you? Haven't you been listening to me at all? My dear girl, I love you. That's why you must go away."

"Love me?" Cara felt stupid with her inability to understand.

For answer Julian pulled her against his chest, bending his head to her ashen face. His kiss was excruciating gentle as he tried to communicate his love for her without words. Cara was stunned momentarily; then her heart expanded at the wonder of his words, as their meaning finally penetrated her brain. Her senses fired at his touch. Blissfully Cara melted against him, reaching up to circle his neck with her arms. With a groan of despair, Julian tore her arms down and pushed her away.

"Now, do you see why it's impossible? I couldn't keep my hands off you if you were to remain in England."

He flung himself down on the wooden bench. His breathing was ragged as he fought for control. Puzzled by his behavior and even more confused by his words, Cara stared down at him in motionless dismay. Then suddenly her eyes opened wide and she expelled her breath in a sigh of pure pleasure. She knelt down at Julian's feet, taking his hands in her own. Putting them against her cheek, she scanned his anguished face.

"Please, Julian, don't be angry with me. At least, not yet," Cara cautioned with a guilty laugh. "You say you came to the duchess to ask for an annulment of your marriage. Why, Julian?"

"Because I had fallen in love with you," he stated flatly.

Cara closed her eyes, bending her head to kiss his hands. Then glancing up into his beloved face, she smiled. It was a smile of such infinite sweetness that Julian found his own heart swelling with love.

"Did you tell Her Grace why you wanted an annulment?"

"I tried. I couldn't seem to be able to explain it very well." Julian clutched at Cara's hands by way of apology at his own inadequacies. "It had never mattered before whom I married. What little I had seen of marital bliss was a sham. I had never met a woman I could either love or trust. And then you came storming into my peaceful life."

Julian's dark head bent to Cara's burnished curls, and he kissed the silken strands. Then, tipping her head, he kissed her softly on the lips.

"You annoyed me. You angered me. You frustrated me at every turn. You took over my household, made me burn with desire, and had the audacity to criticize my behavior toward the children."

180

Cara had the good grace to look slightly shamefaced, but Julian did not fail to spot the mischievous smile at the corners of her mouth.

"You ran from me in the woods, and I searched for you all over the county. And there you sat, night after night, in the schoolroom, telling stories and embroidering some infernal chair cover. I must have been blind."

"But I didn't want you to find me," Cara declared indignantly.

Defiantly she met Julian's black-browed glare. Then, ignoring the interruption, he continued.

"You were everywhere I looked. And when I didn't see you, I thought about you. First it was in anger; then in frustrated desire. And finally with love," he finished quietly.

The two of them were silent. Cara was the first to break the spell of enchantment around them. Her question jolted Julian back to the present.

"What did the duchess say about the annulment?"

"She said it was impossible," Julian replied furiously. "She even had the gall to ask me if I intended to make you my mistress."

"Do you, Julian?" Cara asked curiously.

"I could never treat you shabbily, my dear," he answered. "I do love you so, but I could never permit you to become the topic of malicious gossip. It seems our honor stands in the way of our love."

His last words were spoken ironically as he brought her hand to his lips. Gazing down at the exquisite girl at his feet, he was proud of his decision, no matter how much it hurt. Cara's face glowed with pride and her eyes touched him with love.

"So you see, my dear, this is good-bye. I was sent out here to wait for my wife. Unaccountably, I found you instead."

It was Cara's turn to feel fear. She had listened to Julian's declaration without thought of the eventual outcome. Now it was time for her to confess. In her heart Cara suspected that her revelations would not be met with the same joy in which she had received Julian's confidences.

"Julian, do you swear that you love me?" Cara begged earnestly.

"Of course I do. But it solves nothing in our present damnable situation."

"Even if I tell you that I've done something so terrible that you may have trouble forgiving me?"

"Ah, sweetheart, you could never have done anything that dreadful." He patted Cara's shoulder as though consoling a distraught child.

"But I have, Julian. You see, I am your wife," she blurted out.

"You're what?" Julian shook his head in bewilderment.

"I am your wife," Cara repeated. "The duchess's granddaughter. I am Caroline Leland."

Julian stared at Cara in stupefaction, unable to understand her meaning at first. Slowly his eyes narrowed, and she turned away from the penetrating brown eyes that bored into her heart. He jerked his hands away from her. Jumping to his feet, he glared down at the abject girl, crumpled like a wilted flower.

"Do you mean to tell me you wormed your way into my household under false pretenses?" he thundered.

Cara flinched as his angry words pounded at her. Now that she had confessed, her bravery deserted her completely, and she cowered at Julian's feet.

"Yes, Julian, but . . ."

"And all the time you were preaching at me about the honesty of Americans?" He whirled around, striking out at the pillar of the gazebo. "What a mockery. You must have laughed into your hand at the spectacle I was making."

He stormed to the far side and leaned on the railing,

staring out over the duchess's lush gardens. Scrambling to her feet, Cara ran after him, stopping in dismay as she faced the rigid wall of his back.

"Oh, Julian, it was never like that. Please believe me," she argued. "I was desperate. I was married to a man I had never seen. All I wanted was to find out a little about you before we were forced to begin our married life." Disconsolately she stared at his rigid figure.

As Julian continued to turn from her, Cara felt a frisson of fear, but then she remembered what little choice she had at the time. Her voice, which had been pleading, took on a note of indignation at the injustice of her situation.

"Perhaps you have a right to be angry. But all I intended to do was just to observe you. I was to stay in the background and then was to return here. And you would never have known." Cara waited for a moment, hoping for some sign of thawing, then at his continued silence, found herself once more furious with him. "Besides, you were so hateful at first, I just couldn't keep quiet. The children needed me to speak up for them."

Julian turned, his eyes taking in Cara's angry expression. It seemed strange that he had never even considered what his bride would feel on her arrival in England. He had given so little thought to the marriage. Looking down at Cara, he was suffused with fury, but this time at his own insensitivity. Gently he gathered her into his arms.

"My darling girl, I never realized what an awful prospect our marriage was for you."

"But, you see, I made a pretty mess of everything," Cara said softly. "I had come to love you, Julian. If I could have just remained uninvolved, everything would have been well."

Cara's eyes brimmed with tears of love and joy that overflowed as she reached up to encircle his neck. With infinite care, Julian bent to kiss her tearstained cheeks. He tasted the salt and followed the trail of moisture to the corner of her mouth where he nibbled contentedly for a moment. He smiled tenderly at the girl in his arms.

"It wouldn't have all gone well, my dear, because by that time I had fallen in love with a saucy termagant who tyrannized my household."

Cara had the grace to blush at his teasing. Then, tipping her head to the side, she quirked an eyebrow up at him.

"Do you mind very much, milord?"

Julian's lips told her how little he minded. But suddenly he pushed her away and stared at her, a frown wrinkling his forehead.

"It's getting very confusing, you know. Miss Farraday. Caroline Leland. And now I'll have to learn another name. But Lady Wilton does become you."

Unabashedly the duchess stood at the window watching as Julian bent his head to kiss the lovely girl in his arms. A smile of remembrance appeared at the corners of her mouth as she recalled her own romance. Cara was definitely going to brighten up the dull days ahead, the older woman thought. Perhaps she would soon be seeing a great-grandchild. If only the child had red hair and a temper, the duchess would be well satisfied.

Regency presents the popular and prolific...
JOAN SMITH

Allow at least 4 weeks for delivery.
TAF-67